KU-778-222

We are GOING *to a*
WEDDING

ROBERT DAVIES HIGGINS

Leabharlanna Poiblí Chathair Baile Átha Cliath
Dublin City Public Libraries

Withdrawn from stock

Dublin Public Libraries

We are Going to a Wedding
Published in 2016 by
AG Books
www.agbooks.co.uk

Typography and layout by
Andrews UK Limited
www.andrewsuk.com

Copyright © 2016 Robert Davies Higgins

The right of Robert Davies Higgins to be identified as author of this book has been asserted in accordance with section 77 and 78 of the Copyrights Designs and Patents Act 1988.

This book is sold subject to the condition that it shall not, by way of trade or otherwise, be lent, resold, hired out or otherwise circulated without the publisher's prior written consent in any form of binding or cover other than that in which it is published, and without a similar condition being imposed on the subsequent purchaser.

All characters appearing in this work are fictitious. Any resemblance to real persons, living or dead, is purely coincidental.

We are GOING to a WEDDING

Brainse Bhaile Thormod
Ballyfermot Library

Tel. 6269324/5

Chapter One

The heat was stifling. Veronica took a deep breath and winced as she felt the hot air searing her lungs.

'I am sorry, Elizabeth, it's no use, I simply cannot stand this heat,' she said. 'I'll have to go out.' She pushed her long auburn curls back from her face as she spoke, and then quickly rose and made her way out of the sauna. A few paces and then the cool welcoming water of the lake enveloped her body in its icy grasp.

She swam for a few minutes, and then came ashore and lay on the grass, feeling so alive and invigorated after her swim. The weather was unusually warm for the time of year, mid-April, and she and her friend Elizabeth Leeson were making the most of their two-day break. They both deserved a rest after their efforts of the last few weeks, preparing their new Craft and Gift Shop for the grand opening'.

The great day was this coming Wednesday. A mere three days away! Veronica shuddered as she thought about the million-and-one tasks still to be done, but neither she nor Elizabeth had any regrets about taking this short break, as they both knew that they would have to work seven days a week for the entire season, and that meant from the end of April right through until the end of October. A very long haul.

The thought of their new enterprise thrilled Veronica every time she thought of it. She had dreamed of this moment for a long time – since she was a child, in fact – and now her dreams were about to be realised. How truly wonderful she was feeling!

Elizabeth was still in the sauna: she did love it, Veronica reflected, but personally she found it to be too hot for her liking.

Brainse Bhaile Thormod
Ballyfermot Library

Tel. 6269324/5

Elizabeth had called her a wimp yesterday when she made a hasty exit. Goodness only knows what she would have to say about today's performance. Wrapping her towel round her, Veronica made her way to her room, where she luxuriated in a delicious hot bubble bath. It was sheer heaven! She dressed in a pair of jeans and a t shirt. She did so hate wearing a bathing costume, and just revelled in donning her clothes once again.

She was of medium height, with hazel eyes, a pert nose and once again felt she was on the dumpy side when she looked in the mirror. Slipping her feet into a comfortable pair of suede pumps, she felt civilised and ready to face the world. She decided to go to the residents' lounge and have tea and scones whilst waiting for Elizabeth.

A nice young Australian girl, who was full of friendly chatter, served her. Veronica chose a pot of Earl Grey tea and a plate of beautiful golden scones, served with butter and whipped cream. The waitress told her that she was 'doing' Europe, had overspent her limited budget when she was in Holland, and was very fortunate to have landed this seasonal job when she arrived in England.

'My name is Cindy Crawford – you know, the same as the super-model,' she said with a wide grin. 'Have you ever been to Holland, especially Amsterdam? Well,' she continued before Veronica could respond, 'you really should make a point of going. It is such a laid-back city – unbelievable!'

Veronica went to speak but Cindy once more got in there first: 'I really blew my mind, and a blooming great hole in my wallet!' She giggled, clearly thinking back. 'But it was worth every penny.'

'Where do you come from, Cindy?' Veronica asked, relieved to get a word in at last.

'I come from Perth in Western Australia, and the one thing I have to do yet while I am still in this country is visit Perth in Scotland, or my old man will never forgive me. He financed the trip. Mind you, I think I will make it there eventually – I don't have to return to Oz until the end of October, just in time to start my final year at uni. I can't wait for graduation.'

'What are you studying?' Veronica asked politely.

'Law, believe it or not'I am sure you will make a fine lawyer someday'

'I doubt that very much. I am only reading Law to suit my dad, else he would never have financed this trip. I wanted to quit last year, but he said if I did, there would be no "doing" Europe at his expense, so naturally I gave in, and the good old boy kept his word and paid my way over here. Still, if by some miracle I pass and get my degree, I reckon that he can be persuaded to let me do the States next.' Cindy sounded philosophical.

"You are an optimist, Cindy,' Veronica said, smiling to herself.

'It should be great fun. I'll talk him into it, no worries! Nice talking to you. I'll have to get back to the kitchen, or it'll be me that will be getting roasted instead of the beef! See you,' she said breezily as she departed for the inner sanctum of the kitchen.

Veronica was still smiling as she savoured the flavours of the scone and lovely dairy butter, freshly made strawberry jam and whipped cream. One thing was for sure, she thought, if a terrific personality had any bearing on achieving success in life, then Cindy Crawford was destined to do as well as her famous namesake. She looked up to see Elizabeth approaching. 'Veronica Shillingworth, when it comes to the question of whom I am going to ask to accompany me on my trip to the Amazon – when we have made our fortune, that is – don't look in the mirror, girl, because it most certainly won't be you! When it comes to withstanding heat, you are as hopeless as an ice-cream cornet in a blast furnace,' she said teasingly, easing her slim body into the chair, throwing back her golden blond hair looking at her partner with mischievous blue eyes.

'Well, like an ice cream, I remain cool when it counts most, but your conception of a little heat is more akin to a baker's oven. I honestly don't know how you can bear it, Elizabeth.'

'I simply adore it. But then you like a cold frosty morning. Each to their own, Veronica – I hate the cold with a passion.'

'I'll tell you what,' said Veronica. 'When we have made our millions, we'll go to a romantic Caribbean island with white sandy beaches and swaying palm trees, and we will stay in a five-star hotel. You can luxuriate in the tropical heat, and I'll enjoy the air conditioning. How is that for a compromise?'

'Fantastic! Now I know why we are such good partners.

I get an odd idea now and again, and you have the knack of taking a mundane proposition and turning it into something quite brilliant – what a team!' She flashed her dazzling smile.

'Would you care for a cup of Earl Grey?' Veronica asked.

'Yes please After all, it is the nearest thing to having contact with a male since we arrived.'

'You are the limit, Elizabeth Leeson. We are supposed to be here for a nice relaxing break, not on a man hunt!' Veronica chided.

'Do you mind if I pinch one of your scones?' Elizabeth asked as she helped herself to one. 'You have a nice relaxing break, and I'll have a nice relaxing look, just in case some very fortunate man under the age of ninety happens to stray into this hotel.'

'Ninety? You are obviously far more desperate than I imagined. What did you mean by some "fortunate man", by the way?'

'You are slow at times – he would have the pleasure of meeting yours truly, of course,' came the reply, accompanied by a wicked grin.

'Would you ladies care for more tea or anything?' Cindy asked as she approached their table.

'No thank you, Cindy,' Veronica said. 'By the way, this is my best friend and business partner, Elizabeth Leeson. Elizabeth, meet Cindy Crawford, all the way from Perth, Australia.'

'Pleased to meet you, Cindy.'

'By the way, my name is Veronica Shillingworth. We never got the opportunity to meet properly,' Veronica said quickly before Cindy got a chance to say anything.

'Hi. I am delighted to meet you both. There is such a load of old fuddy-duddies staying in the hotel, it is heaven to speak to people my own age for a change.'

'I bet you don't flinch at the mention of a sauna?' Elizabeth asked the Australian.

'A sauna? I love a sauna! There is a real beaut here – have you tried it yet?'

'I have. Veronica, l am ashamed to say, stuck her nose in for two seconds and bolted. She is frightened she might melt, I think.'

'Very funny,' said Veronica. 'Just you wait till the first time it snows. We'll see who the hardy one is then.'

'Some people can't stand the heat,' Cindy commented philosophically. 'Personally, I love it. I sneaked an hour in the sauna yesterday, and only managed to avoid being caught by the skin of my teeth.' She giggled like a schoolgirl who had almost been caught smoking in the toilets. 'Staff is not allowed to use the facilities, but I can't resist a challenge.'

'I'm with you,' Elizabeth said, 'I'd probably get fired on my first day if I worked here.'

Veronica rose from her chair. 'Well, if you'll excuse me, Elizabeth, I think I'll go for a walk in the grounds. Would you care to join me?' She glanced out of the window as she spoke.

'No thanks, I think I'll stay for a little longer.'

'Wow! Would you look at that!' said Veronica said as she pointed towards the car park.

'Fantastic!' Elizabeth enthused. 'My dreams are coming true.'

'Wow!' Cindy cooed.

A huge old red Cadillac sporting the most enormous tail fins Veronica had ever seen was negotiating into a parking bay.

'Don't tell me that you both actually like that monstrosity?' said Veronica.

'What monstrosity?' they asked in bewilderment.

'The car, of course! How on earth can you drool over that?'

'Stuff the car – I'm drooling over the driver,' Cindy replied, looking at Veronica in astonishment. 'Were you actually looking at the car with a hunk like that before your very eyes? Are you sure you are feeling alright?'

'I saw him first,' Elizabeth said smugly, 'and you know the old adage, "finders keepers".'

'We'll see about that!' Cindy replied, laughing, as they watched the driver emerge from the enormous vehicle.

He stood all of six feet, with blond curly hair and a clean-shaven face.

Broad shoulders carried his black blazer with certain aplomb. A pristine white shirt, worn open-necked with a bright red silk scarf casually tied, gave him an air of casual elegance. A pair of natural pigskin shoes completed his ensemble 'Wow!' Cindy cooed once again, now utterly fascinated.

'He's coming into the hotel,' Elizabeth said in almost a whisper.

'I wonder if he is staying as a guest in the hotel?' Veronica heard herself saying. Why did I say that, she wondered.

'Tell you what,' said Cindy, 'why don't you ladies order another pot of Earl Grey and I'll see what l can find out on the grapevine about out handsome stranger?'

'What a simply marvellous idea! You are a girl after my own heart, Cindy Crawford,' Elizabeth said, bubbling with enthusiasm, pulling the hapless Veronica back into her seat.

'You are beyond the pale at times, Elizabeth. You really can be quite outrageous,' Veronica protested, but secretly she was just as interested as Elizabeth and Cindy in who the handsome stranger was, despite his catastrophic taste in cars.

A few moments later Cindy appeared at their table as if by

magic, carrying the now obligatory tray laden with Earl Grey and a plate heaped with scones.

'Great news – he is staying here for at least a couple of nights. His name is Phillip Marden, and he has pale grey eyes. Tarzan had grey eyes, did you know that? I don't know what he does for a living yet. He is from down south. I don't know exactly where, but I'll try and find out. Hang in there, girls!' And with that last remark, she disappeared into the bowels of the kitchen once again.

'Boy! She is quicker providing information than the internet,' said Elizabeth, marvelling.

'Phillip Marden. That has a certain ring to it, don't you think?' said Veronica. 'Somehow, it just doesn't go hand-in-hand with the impression that one has of someone who drives a monstrosity like that Cadillac.'

'What on earth are you going on about, Veronica? Do you think that because he is driving an old American car that he should be called Evel Knievel? Just because he drives a flash motor doesn't make him Al Capone, you know.'

'No, of course not. I didn't mean to imply that. It's just that the name Phillip Marden sounds so ... English, and his car is so ... American!' She was now feeling rather foolish for having said anything in the first place, and wishing fervently that she hadn't.

'I'll bet its great fun zooming up the M6 in that so-American car,'Elizabeth said. 'As a matter of fact, he probably keeps a Mini like yours in the boot instead of a spare wheel.'

'Very droll, I'm sure. I know that I, for one, prefer my Mini,' Veronica parried haughtily, just a trifle miffed.

'I'll admit that the Mini beats shanks' pony by a country mile,' Elizabeth conceded, adding 'just' under her breath.

A young couple came into the lounge, and Cindy dutifully went to take their order. 'Back in a mo,' she whispered as she passed the girls.

A few moments later she passed by again, this time carrying a tray laden with a pot of tea and pancakes for the couple, whispering 'He's single!' as she swept lightly on her way carrying her burden. She served the couple rather smartly, and then returned to the girls' table.

'Am I good, or am I good?' Before waiting for a reply she immediately continued: 'As I was saying – he's single. On his way to take a new post not too far from here, seemingly. I don't know where yet, but I'll find out soon. His profession is still a mystery. The girls in the kitchen and reception are taking bets on what he is. The odds are: even money his being a doctor, two to one a lawyer, threes he is a teacher. The whole kitty to anyone who guesses correctly if he is anything else. I shouldn't be telling you this, but I thought you might like a little flutter.'

'What a good thought. You are some girl, Cindy! I'll have a pound on him being a doctor. He looks like a doctor. I'll bet he has a great bedside manner,' Elizabeth said.

'I'll bet he has too,' said Cindy, 'but I put my money on a teacher. He looks like an intellectual.'

'I think I'll go for a writer. Definitely a writer,' Veronica said with the air of one who knows.

'As good as done,' Cindy said, palming the money discreetly. 'Would you ladies care to enjoy a few drops of the amber nectar with a poor simple colonial this evening? I get off duty at seven.'

'What a lovely idea,' Veronica said. 'We passed a charming old inn just a few hundred yards from here. Shall we go there?'

'To tell the truth, I had a little bit further in mind. A pub called the Pewter Tankard about eight miles from here,' said Cindy. 'We could take a taxi, so no one has to drive.'

'Surely it makes more sense to walk to the inn?' Veronica suggested.

'I think you are missing out on something slightly subtle, Veronica.' Elizabeth said to her friend.

'Right on, Elizabeth,' said Cindy. 'It just so happens that a certain gent who drives a ... let me see now ... oh yes, a "monstrosity", I am sure I heard it referred to. Well it has come to my notice that the said hunk, sorry, I mean gentleman, is going to the Pewter Tankard this very evening. The landlord of this establishment happens to be his best friend, no less.'

'You are astonishing, Cindy. Where do you get your information? We are definitely having a drop of the golden nectar at the Pewter Tankard tonight. We'll organise a taxi for eight.' Elizabeth bubbled excitedly.

'I will have to meet you outside the gate – staff are not allowed to fraternise with the guests, I'm afraid.'

'Then why don't we meet at the inn down the road, and take a taxi from there, away from prying eyes?' Veronica suggested.

Everyone agreed to this sensible arrangement just as the maître'd appeared, and Cindy beat a hasty retreat to the kitchen.

Phillip was in deep conversation with his lifelong friend Tim Jones-Belling, and did not notice the three attractive young women entering the lounge bar and occupying the table to his left.

'I really love it here,' Tim was saying to Phillip. 'One becomes accustomed quite quickly to the long hours that the pub demands – much to my amazement. Not to mention the people you meet from all walks of life, and all nationalities. I don't know why I didn't do this years ago, Phillip.'

'So you are settling in well then – I am glad. I honestly never thought you would.'

'I find this life far more satisfying than selling stocks and bonds. Staring at a computer screen all day every day gets a wee bit wearing, to say the least. Best move I ever made.'

'I am delighted for you, Tim. I honestly thought that you had made a fatal error when you told me that you had bought a pub, especially in the Yorkshire Dales. I thought you had lost your marbles. I gave you three months at most, before you were back in London with your tail between your legs. I admit that I was wrong. I'll take my portion of humble pie now, please,' Phillip said, bowing his head.

'Very big of you, old chap, but humble pie won't be necessary. I was not entirely certain that I had done the right thing myself. However, I have no such doubts about your own move here. You will take to country life like a duck to water.'

'I hope you're right. I do admit that I had no qualms when I was offered the post. I always loved it when we were kids and spent our summers at the estate. My ambition has always been to earn a living that allowed me to live in the country. This is the first opportunity that has presented itself. I grabbed it with both hands.'

'You'll do just fine,' said Tim 'If anyone can make it succeed, you can. The position is perfect for you. It will be nice having you close by.'

A waitress arrived with their meals. Phillip had ordered English roast beef with all the trimmings, including – of course – Yorkshire pudding and roast potatoes. Tim decided on a salad. He had been in the kitchen most of the day, and like many cooks when preparing the food, he was prone to sampling his handiwork, in his case rather too frequently, so he opted for the less fattening main meal.

'This beef is quite delicious,' Phillip commented as he ate with gusto. 'I never realised how hungry I was – in fact I'm ravenous. Come to think about it, I haven't actually eaten since breakfast. That was at five-thirty this morning.'

'No wonder you're hungry. I suggest you indulge yourself with a helping of Spotted Dick for dessert.

Absolutely guaranteed to quell the pangs of hunger .'

'Spotted Dick?' Phillip laughed. 'How could I resist? Tell me – do you do some of the cooking yourself?'

'Most of it, actually,' came the unexpected reply.

'You do surprise me. I never knew you could cook. The food is really first class. Congratulations are in order,' Phillip said sincerely.

'Thank you, Phillip. Praise indeed! I do appreciate it. Makes me feel I am actually achieving something, and not just playing out a fantasy.'

'You're welcome, and I meant every word.' He popped the last morsel of Yorkshire pudding into his mouth.

As Phillip tackled his dessert, Tim took the opportunity to do his duty and take a stroll round the pub to check on things. Immediately his eye was taken by the three young ladies seated at the table to his left. How on earth had he and Phillip missed them coming in? Must be getting old, he thought. Unconsciously he straightened his tie and went over to introduce himself to the girls.

Veronica, Elizabeth and Cindy, preoccupied with sorting out the for their drinks, did not notice Tim as he approached and were very pleasantly surprised when they heard a deep male voice say 'Good evening, ladies. Everything to your satisfaction?'

'Yes, thank you,' Veronica replied as she looked up and saw the dark-haired chap who had been sitting with Phillip Marden. He sported a huge friendly grin, revealing a row of perfect straight teeth.

'I am Tim Jones-Belling, proprietor of this establishment, and I am at your service,' he said, beaming.

'Good on you, mate. The service and the beer are real beaut, thanks,' Cindy said.

'Oh-ho. I see we have a visitor from the Antipodes. My friend was over there recently. He has only been back a few weeks.' He turned to call over to the next table. 'Phillip, when were you in Australia?'

'I was there all of January and the most of February. Why?' he asked, without looking up, preoccupied with the dessert.

'Cindy is from Australia. I thought perhaps you may know her home town,' Tim said, willing Phillip away from his pudding and hopefully to coax him into the conversation.

'Australia is a very large country, Tim, so it is highly unlikely. Where are you from, Cindy?' he asked as he turned to face them reluctantly, was suddenly very pleased that he had done so when he saw three pretty girls opposite.

'Perth in Western Australia. Do you know it?'

'What a coincidence – that is where I have just come from. Quite a place! I was down for the Americas Cup trials. A really beautiful city, and the people are so friendly. I don't think I held an empty glass all the time I was there. Everyone kept plying me with beer. It was terrific.' He smiled at the memory. 'By the way, I'm Phillip Marden.'

'Hi, Phillip. I'm Cindy, and this is Veronica and Elizabeth.'

'Very nice to meet you. Are you ladies from Perth as well?'

'No,' Elizabeth replied, glad to gain Phillip's attention.

'Veronica and I are English. Excuse me, but didn't I see you at the Grand Manor Hotel earlier today?'

'That is quite possible. I booked in there today. I'll be staying for a few days.'

'So are we,' Elizabeth said. 'I thought I recognised you. That's quite a car you drive.'

'You spotted the old Cadillac, then?' he replied, smiling like a Cheshire cat. 'It is hard to miss, right enough, but as you say, quite a car!'

'A thing like that is rather hard to miss,' Veronica interjected, and regretted saying so immediately. He no doubt thought her extremely sarcastic.

'Oh-oh. The lady does not approve of my taste in automobiles. This particular car has a very special history. That reminds me – when I was in Perth, Cindy, I saw another interesting American car. The same vintage as mine, but this one was a Chrysler

Imperial. What a car!'

'A peculiar brownish sort of grey colour?' Cindy asked.

'Yes. You obviously know it then. Isn't that amazing!

The chap who owns it was courteous enough to give me a ride in it. Absolutely splendid vehicle. He was a nice chap, called Crawford. I don't suppose you know him, by any chance?'

'Would that be Tom Crawford, about six one, going bald?'

'Totally amazing! You do know him?'

'Mm. Just ever so slightly – he's my father!' Cindy replied, smiling.

They were all agreed – an absolutely wonderful evening had been enjoyed by everyone. The old Cadillac simply purred silently along, and even Veronica had to admit that it was probably the most comfortable car ride she had ever experienced.

Phillip had insisted on driving the girls back to the hotel, and would not take no for an answer. Elizabeth and Cindy were ever so slightly tipsy, but Veronica had been much more circumspect, as per usual. She always drank alcohol in moderation, and no amount of cajoling or persuasion could make her change her mind.

Phillip had only had soft drinks all evening, as he was driving. He had mentioned that he had an important appointment in the morning, and he had deliberately taken the car to the pub, knowing that Tim would not try to cajole him into taking a drink when he was driving, thus guaranteeing a clear head, not to mention a clean licence in the morning.

'You must be quite a yachtsman to go all the way to Australia just to see the Americas Cup Trials,' Cindy said.

'Well, I have done a little sailing in my time, but not in that league. Those sailors are just a tad above my ken, I'm afraid. I was very lucky – the editor of a leading yachting magazine is a good friend, and the fellow that was contracted to cover the Trials fell off a ladder in his home, believe it or not. Poor chap broke his hip. My friend had to find an immediate replacement for the poor bugger, and very kindly offered the assignment to me. Naturally, after considering it for at least a split second, I jumped at the chance. I had never covered a yacht race before, but he published my articles verbatim, so they must have come across as reasonably professional, and the money was excellent.'

'You are a reporter – wow! That must be exciting,' Elizabeth said in a rather thick voice, slightly slurred with the effects of the alcohol she had consumed.

'No, I am a writer, actually, but one cannot afford to cock a snoot at magazine work, especially when it involves foreign travel and a handsome pay check to boot,' he replied cheerfully.

Cindy nudged Veronica in the ribs and whispered 'I'll collect your winnings in the morning.'

'What was that you said?' Phillip asked.

'I was just asking Veronica if she fancied going swimming in the morning,' Cindy lied, thinking quickly. Veronica felt her face flush, terrified that Cindy would let it slip about the bet. Her face was on fire.

'You are the one who said that you would never be seen dead in a car like this,' said Elizabeth, collapsing in a fit of giggles. 'And now you are sitting in the front seat as though you were the Duchess of Cambridge!'

'I never said anything of the sort, Elizabeth Leeson,' Veronica protested, her face burning even brighter.

'This old beauty has royal credentials, I'll have you know, and Elizabeth is correct on one score, Veronica – you do have the grace of a princess. A fairy tale princess at that, if I may be so bold to say so,' Phillip said, in a gentle warm voice. Veronica blushed to her roots.

'Wow!' Cindy cooed in a whisper.

'If Veronica teases me, will I get pampered by you too?' Elizabeth asked Phillip in devilment.

'So long as you both realise that you were being unkind to Veronica. Remember, sarcasm is the lowest form of humour,' Phillip chided.

'Sorry Veronica,' said Elizabeth. 'We didn't mean to embarrass you.'

'No offence taken,' she answered, waving over her shoulder to her friend. She suddenly burst into fits of laughter. 'Now you have me waving like royalty!' she declared, and they all laughed heartily. They fell into silence for a little while, as is often the case after a bout of laughter, each lost in their own thoughts.

Elizabeth gave a contented sigh as her thoughts strayed to Tim. There was no question about it – she had had her sights well and truly set on Phillip from the outset of the evening, but the longer she had spent in Tim's company, the more she had become attracted to him. No matter that she had scolded herself severely for allowing her attentions to be distracted from the blond handsome Phillip; those big brown eyes and a smile full of devilment drew her to Tim like a magnet. This had never happened to her – it was an utterly new experience. She was well and truly caught, hook line and sinker. It was love and it was a wonderful feeling.

Tim had asked her to dinner the following Saturday, and Veronica had been a dear and had very kindly agreed to Elizabeth leaving early that evening from the shop.

Chapter Two

'We have arrived,' Phillip announced as he negotiated the large vehicle into a parking space. Cindy thanked one and all for a 'beaut' evening, and then ran to the side of the building and slipped quietly into the staff entrance.

Phillip invited Veronica and Elizabeth to join him in the residents' lounge for coffee, but Elizabeth declined, saying she had better call it a day, and tactfully retired, bidding them a good night. Veronica accepted the offer, feeling it would be rude not to. He was a strikingly handsome man, she noted as he politely pulled her chair clear of the table, and such good manners too.

'You said your car has royal credentials – you were joking of course?' Veronica asked, desperate to make conversation on a subject that she knew he was interested in, afraid that he would otherwise find her boring, and bring the evening to a premature end. Her mother had always told her that she was prone to be rather dull and tedious at times (unlike her younger sister, Melanie, who had a wonderful natural laid-back attitude) and had advised Veronica to speak only when spoken to in male company, for her own good, and to let the man lead the conversation. Naturally, mother always added that she could not imagine, for the life of her, from whom Veronica could have inherited such a dull personality.

Thus, poor Veronica had grown up with rather an inferiority complex, no thanks to her mother, and as a result usually remained rather timid in company – especially male company. But with this devastatingly handsome man all to herself, at least for the next few minutes, she simply had to suppress her shyness. She knew he liked her, and hopefully he would command the conversation.

16

"This old girl has a wonderful pedigree. It really is a long story, though, and I would hate to run the risk of boring you with it, Veronica," he said.

'Please tell me. Honestly, I am genuinely interested. You have made it sound so intriguing, and you can't leave it there, Phillip – please.'

'Don't say I didn't warn you,' he replied with a warm smile. 'My dad worked for an extremely wealthy royal family from the Middle East. Well, that is not entirely accurate – he still works for the family, but the person who owned the car passed away a couple of years ago. Dad actually worked for him, but decided to stay on at the family's request. He is a chartered accountant, and he is the business manager for the Sultan's European interests.'

He paused to take a sip of coffee. 'I did warn you that it is boring.'

'No, I find it fascinating. Please go on.'

'Tim's father is their racing stable manager. We get great tips from him!' He flashed a wicked smile. 'Now where was I? Oh yes. The Sultan owned several houses in Britain, one of which is Brinsdale, a stately house in the Cotswolds. Tim and I spent our summer holidays there as kids, as did Crown Prince Naseem, who is the same age as us. We had a great time. No, I haven't forgotten about the car. I am just filling in the necessary background.'

'I didn't think for a moment that you had forgotten, Phillip,' Veronica said. 'It is truly fascinating.'

'You have heard of President John F Kennedy? What a silly question. Of course you have!' He berated himself before she could reply. 'A little-known fact is that Kennedy was planning a visit to this country, part official, part private.' He took another sip of coffee. '

The private part of the visit was that the Kennedyswere to have stayed at Brinsdale. They were personal friends of the Sultan, close friends actually, stemming from university days. Would you care for more coffee?' He lifted the silver coffee pot as he spoke, and refilled their cups.

'Thank you,' Veronica whispered.

'To continue. The Sultan decided to present his friend with a gift. A gift worthy of a President. Suitable but extravagant. He decided on a car and ordered a Cadillac made to his own specifications. Did you notice anything special when you were in the car?'

'No, apart from the sheer size, I cannot honestly say that I did,' she replied, kicking herself for not having been more observant.

'I'll give you a hint – the steering.'

'No. It looked perfectly normal to me.' she said, frantically searching her mind's eye, picturing the car's interior, and drawing a blank.

'Exactly!' he enthused. 'Don't you see? An American car that appears perfectly normal to you, an Englishwoman?'

'Of course!' Veronica replied, the light suddenly dawning. 'The steering wheel is on the right hand side.' She felt such a fool for not having realised that.

'Well done! The Sultan had right hand steering installed when it was built. I have been told that there is only one other of that model to have been built specifically for the British roads, and that was for the American ambassador.'

He said it with just a hint of pride.

He made to refill their cups once more, only to discover to his amazement that the pot was empty. 'I never realised we had drunk so much,' he said. 'Would you care for more? I know I certainly would.' He was signalling the waiter as he spoke.

'Yes please,' she replied, eager to remain in his company, no matter how many cups of coffee she had to drink.

'Are you really positive that you are not just being polite? I am usually accused of boring people to the point of committing suicide when it comes to the subject of the Cadillac, and I would hate to be responsible for your untimely demise,' he said, teasing.

'I've told you already, Phillip. I am genuinely interested. I would not say so if I didn't mean it,' Veronica reassured him.

'I believe you. The Cadillac was duly delivered to England, and then ... well, we all know what happened in Dallas. The Sultan never had the pleasure of presenting his friend with his gift. The car was put in a garage at Brinsdale, where it lay untouched for thirty years.'

'How sad.'

'Yes, it is sad, really. When I was a boy, I used to sneak into the garage and spend hours sitting behind the wheel, pretending that I was driving the President of the USA to Buckingham Palace to meet the Queen. JFK would be so thrilled with my skill as a driver, he would present me with a Purple Heart medal every time. The Purple Heart was, of course, the only American decoration I had heard of as a boy.' He smiled as he remembered his childhood fantasies with fondness.

'In my imaginings I had a drawer full of medals that would have made even Rambo positively green with 'You certainly did not lack imagination, but I think it was so sweet! Did Tim share in your secret?' she asked.

'Good grief, no. That was my own little world. Mind you, John Kennedy was assassinated many years before I was even born. I guess I must have had a slightly more vivid imagination than most kids,' he confessed.

'Vivid, yes, but I think that Kennedy is such a legend, familiar to everyone. To tell the truth, I could very easily imagine him in the car myself, now. I guess that makes me as daft as you. No, it's even worse – you have the excuse of having been only a child!'

Phillip laughed with her. 'I think that you do understand how I feel about the silly thing. Most of my friends are convinced that I am nuts.'

'You can tell them then that you have at least one sympathiser.'

'The car was kept fully operational, of course. But it never left the grounds of the estate. Simply serviced and then returned to the garage,' he continued.

'It never left the grounds even once? That is amazing.

Imagine – all that time. You would think that the Sultan would have sold it.'

'I was at the estate about three years ago for a few days visiting my parents. As usual I went to the garage to see the car. Sentimental and a bit silly, I suppose, but it was like visiting an old friend,' he freely admitted.

'I don't think you're silly. I think my little Mini has a personality of her own. You see, I am as silly as a lot of people – I refer to my car as 'she'.'

'Good for you!' Phillip replied. 'I have always found cars to have a personality – there is just something about them one cannot explain. Uncanny, really.'

'How did you acquire the Cadillac?' Veronica prompted.

'Sorry. As I was saying, I went to the garage to see the car. When I returned to the house, the Sultan sent for me. He told me that he used to observe me as a child, spending many hours in the car. I was stunned by this. I never knew that anyone had ever seen me. To say I was embarrassed was an understatement.' He paused to sip some welcome coffee. The Sultan said:

"Don't be embarrassed, Phillip. You committed no wrong-doing – you were a child, and you were doing what made you happy, and a happy child is a blessing indeed from Allah." I thought that was extremely nice of him. He then went on to ask if I now coveted the car, and if I had any idea as to its value. I told him I had never even thought of it having any value, but now that he had mentioned it, I said I guess it must have. I told him that I looked on the car as an old friend, and not as an object of value or envy.

'He said that was as he thought, and to my utter astonishment, he handed me the keys, saying that he had bought it for a special friend, but Allah had willed that the car find its own special friend, and it had.' Phillip was obviously very moved as he recalled that moment. His eyes actually filled with tears.

'I was very privileged. Now you perhaps understand why the car is so special to me. I am probably the only man in Britain who can relive his childhood every time he gets behind the driving wheel. It is magical.'

'What a fabulous story! I am glad that you shared it with me, Phillip. I promise I will look at the Cadillac with respect from now on,' Veronica replied, grinning widely, secretly thrilled that Phillip had told her his romantic tale.

'I forgot to ask how long you and Elizabeth are staying. A few days yet, I hope.'

'I wish that we were. Unfortunately we must return home tomorrow. Our new craft shop opens in three days, and we still have a few last-minute things to do,' she replied with a touch of sadness.

'What a shame. I have an appointment in Harrogate in the morning – a business breakfast. I hope to be back here for lunchtime. Can you stay until then? I'll treat you both to lunch.'

'I am sure we can stay on for lunch – thank you. Did you actually say that you are having a business breakfast? I have never heard of that before. What an extraordinary idea!' Veronica said.

'My appointment is with Americans. Business breakfast is a common occurrence in the States. They work harder than we British, I think. They are firm believers in the early bird catching the worm, and all that,' he replied, smiling broadly.

'I still think it a strange idea,' Veronica said with a little shake of her head.

'We have a firm date for lunch tomorrow?'

'Absolutely. I hope your breakfast meeting goes well for you,' she said, unconsciously touching his hand.

'Thank you. I am walking on thin ice really, I have taken on a position that I am not sure I am competent enough to handle. I just hope I have not made a serious error.' He frowned slightly.

'You don't strike me as someone who would be incompetent at anything you put your mind to, Phillip.'

'Thanks for the vote of confidence,' he replied with a broad smile. 'I'll let you know tomorrow if it is justified.'

The next morning Phillip left the hotel very early. He did not see Veronica looking out of her window watching the Cadillac silently cruise down the driveway. He had not confided in her as to what the position he had accepted was, or what he was expected to do, or why he was now not so sure he was the right person for this. Perhaps he would do so when he returned.

Elizabeth slept until nine o'clock but Veronica had decided to stay up after she watched Phillip leave and she went for a long walk in the country. It was a beautiful morning, the birds were singing, and she thoroughly enjoyed the cool air and the early morning sun.

Cindy was on duty when she arrived back at the hotel and went to the dining room for breakfast. A full English breakfast was the order of the day for Veronica; she did enjoy breakfast when she was on holiday, but rarely ate one when she was at home. Strange person I am, she thought as she tucked in to her bacon and eggs.

Elizabeth finally appeared, and surprised Veronica when all she had was coffee. 'I have a bit of a hangover, I am ashamed to say,' she confided. 'I have a favour to ask, Veronica. Would you mind terribly if we stayed on until the evening? I meant to tell you last night, but I succumbed to the alcohol, I am afraid, and I forgot to ask. I made a date to meet Tim today for lunch. He is driving over here.

I am sorry I didn't mention it last night.' she said apologetically.

Veronica suddenly started laughing. 'That is funny, Elizabeth. I was about to ask you the same thing! Phillip asked us to lunch, and I agreed on both our accounts. I was sure you wouldn't object. Now we can all have lunch together, if that is all right with you.'

'That's great. I am sure the boys won't object either.

Has Phillip been down for breakfast yet?'

'Phillip went to Harrogate this morning. He had an early appointment. A breakfast … no, that is wrong … a business breakfast meeting, would you believe!' Veronica was still amused by this concept.

'I believe you. I bet he was meeting with Americans.'

'How on earth did you know that? Tim must have told you,' Veronica said.

'No, honestly – Tim never mentioned Phillip. Surely you must know that the business breakfast is all the rage in the States? I just put two and two together when you told me he was having a business breakfast.'

'I must lead a very sheltered existence. I had never heard of it until Phillip told me last night. It looks like I must be the only one who hasn't.' Veronica felt slightly miffed that she seemed to be so far behind the times.

' You rarely go to the cinema. If you did, you would certainly have heard the expression used many times. Surely you don't think that I am developing some semblance of intelligence at this late stage in life? Did you think that I had broken a lifetime's habit and started reading? Silly girl,' she scolded.

'You are the limit, Elizabeth. I wonder if Cindy is free this afternoon?'

'I'll pop out to the restroom and try and have a word with her. She seems to be restricted to the other side of the dining room this morning.' Elizabeth rose from the table as she spoke and made her way across the room. She managed to catch Cindy as she finished serving an Austrian couple who spoke poor English, and Cindy had been attempting to help with the menu using sign language. There had been a flood of giggles from the table, and the maître'd had intervened, annoyed at the giggling, and blaming his itinerant waitress, whom he regarded as just slightly better than hopeless. He, being a fluent German speaker, soon solved the Austrians' choice, and dispatched Cindy to fetch their order. The couple thanked her when she returned with their food, and gave her a large smile and a wink. She felt rather pleased with herself, and dismissed from her mind the rollicking that she had received in the kitchen.

Elizabeth asked her in a low whisper if she was free in the afternoon, and was delighted when Cindy said that she was. They hurriedly arranged to meet in the local pub after lunch at two o'clock.

The foursome had a delightful time together as they enjoyed a fresh smoked salmon salad for lunch. Laughter rang out as both Tim and Phillip reminisced their about childhood escapades, keeping Veronica and Elizabeth in stitches.

'I think it is time we were heading for the pub – we wouldn't want to keep Cindy waiting,' Veronica said.

'We'll have to decide on whose car we are going in.'

Phillip said: 'We can go down in one car – it makes a lot more sense than using three of them.'

They all agreed, and after a. bit of discussion, Tim won and they used his Mercedes. Elizabeth sat in the front with Tim, and Veronica and Phillip shared the back seat.

'You haven't told us how your meeting went, old boy,' Tim remarked.

'Rather well, actually. I'm still not sure if I have made the right decision, but I am fully committed now.'

'You'll do just fine. You are a natural for the job. The TV camera will love you. Three months from now we will have to make an appointment to see you. Becoming a star will make you so big-headed you probably won't want to associate with us mere mortals.' Tim liked teasing his friend.

'You are going into television?' Elizabeth said, very impressed. 'I have never met anyone who actually worked in television. How exciting. Don't you think it's exciting, Veronica?'

'I am sure it must be exciting for Phillip. It sounds a wonderful opportunity.'

'See what you have started, Tim,' said Phillip. 'I have been given a contract by an American satellite TV company to do a series of fishing programmes, to be shown in the middle of the night in this country. The show is aimed at the States, really. I'll be covering fishing in Europe and Russia.

'The Russians are going into the sports pursuits in a big way, chasing the dollar, of course. I am sure very few people will watch it here, considering the hour it is to be broadcast. I'll hardly become a star, but 1 will certainly get some great travel opportunities over the next two years. I am looking forward to that.'

'Are you to write your own scripts?' Veronica asked.

'Yes. That's the reason I finally agreed to take the job. Plus the fact that it also allows me a considerable amount of free time and freedom of contract to write articles for magazines etcetera. Ideal, really,' he said with a wide grin.

'You are a crafty old fox. I'll bet you have contracts lined up with sporting magazines to run articles on the places you go to for the programme,' Tim speculated.

'How did you guess?' came the reply, Phillip's grin widening even more.

'I knew it!' Tim said with a satisfied smirk. 'I just knew it.'What exactly will you be doing, Phillip? Do you have to go fishing, and hope that the fish jump onto your hook for the benefit of the camera?' Veronica asked. 'I have never watched a fishing programme on television, so I don't know what they actually do. How can you possibly make it interesting? I am not trying to belittle you, it's just that fishing always struck me as a very boring pastime. I'm sorry, I know I'm going on a bit, but I really am interested in what you are expected to do keep your audience's attention.'

'That is a very good question. I am not too sure myself at the moment, and that is the truth. I wrote a few articles for an angling magazine last year – I have always been a keen angler. The producer of the American TV company read them and – much to my surprise – offered me the job hosting their new fishing in Europe programme. I am expected to fish myself, of course, but each week a guest angler will be invited to accompany me to a river or lake somewhere in Europe. I am hoping the guests prove to be the experts they supposedly are. Otherwise I can envisage a lot of side trips to freezer departments in the supermarkets!' he said with a laugh.

Cindy was already there when they arrived, and greeted them with a huge smile. 'I was on the phone to my dad before I came out. He said I've to tell you, Phillip, that you owe him a bottle of beer, and if you took the job you owe him a case of the stuff.'

Everyone looked at Phillip, who started laughing. 'You know he's right. He bet me a case of beer against a bottle that I would run into his daughter when I returned to England. I thought he was nuts. No offence, Cindy. He just smiled and said that if he knew his daughter, she would find someone who had been to Perth. He said that if you didn't trip over me you would probably fall over me and that you have an uncanny knack. He bet me I would take the TV job. I was sure then that I wouldn't.'

'If I know my old man, he'll probably turn up at your door some night to collect his winnings, so you had better stock up on the old amber nectar, Phillip,' Cindy said with a serious expression, giving the girls a crafty wink.

'Then I had better get a stock in when I move into my new cottage,' Phillip replied. 'I would hate Tom to come all the way from Australia to an empty fridge.'

'Good on you, Phillip. By the way. I think my dad's words were that he was sure that I would probably bump into you in England … that if he knew his daughter, she wouldn't fail to meet a hunk like you!

Chapter Three

'I really appreciate it, Veronica,' said Elizabeth, picking up her coat and moving towards the shop door. I always seem to be leaving early – are you sure that you don't mind?'

'Of course not, Elizabeth. You know as well as I do that it is quiet, to say the least. I do wish this awful weather would improve.'

'This is England. We all know the weather can be inclement for long stretches. I guess we have to accept that when the weather is as bad in this neck of the woods as it has been, trade is correspondingly bad too, unfortunately.' Elizabeth sounded philosophical.

'I know that's true, but it's very frustrating neve the – less. Time for a coffee before you leave?' asked Veronica, changing the subject.

'Oh go on then – yes please,' she said, putting down her coat.

Veronica filled the kettle.

'You and Tim have been seeing quite a lot of each other. Are you getting serious?'

'Well … to be totally honest, yes we are. I never thought it could happen to me, but there you are!' She shrugged her shoulders in surrender. 'Does it surprise you?'

'No. A blind man could see that you are crazy about each other. I am glad for you and Tim.'

'You know, there is something I have been meaning to ask you since we were at the hotel. How on earth did you guess that Phillip was a writer? It has puzzled me.'

'Ah. Elementary, my dear Watson,' Veronica replied, picking up a hand-carved pipe from a small display case, and trying her best to mimic Sherlock Holmes. 'You see, he was carrying a big stack of yachting magazines under his arm when he walked from his car to the hotel. Simple really.'

'I never noticed that. How could I miss something so obvious?' complained Elizabeth.

'The answer to that question is simple too. You and Cindy were preoccupied admiring his broad shoulders and blond curls.'

'True! But each to their own set of priorities!' said Elizabeth, smugly.

'Speaking of Cindy, I wonder how she is getting on.' Veronica said. 'She is such a nice girl, and such good fun too.'

'Yes, it would be lovely to hear from her, but I guess she has been kept busy at work. I dare say that the hotel is busier than we are, despite the weather. But it would be nice to hear from her again.'

'You know, we should phone the hotel and invite her over on her day off. I could fetch her in the car.'

'That would be fun. I've a great idea. Let's phone her right now.' Elizabeth said enthusiastically.

'Great – you phone and I'll make the coffee. Do you fancy a chocolate biscuit?' Veronica asked as she spooned instant coffee granules into the cups.

'Why ever not? Let's be devils for once,' Elizabeth replied as she dialled the hotel's number.

Veronica entered the front shop carrying two steaming cups of coffee and two chocolate biscuits wrapped in bright red foil, hiding the chocolate heaven, cloaked in sinful scarlet.

Elizabeth was just replacing the receiver as Veronica placed the cups on the counter. 'Cindy left her job in the hotel over two weeks ago. She didn't leave a forwarding address,' Elizabeth said, unable to hide her obvious disappointment.

'Oh. I do hope she gets in touch before she returns to Australia. I would hate to lose contact with her.'

'I'm sure she will contact us, Veronica. I'll bet you she makes a point of coming to see us. Now, come on, cheer up, and **let's** be really decadent and investigate how thick the chocolate is covering these biscuits.

'Delicious. Are you and Tim going out for a meal, or are you eating at the pub?'

'We're going to a restaurant in Harrogate, actually. He has an appointment with a solicitor which he said will take about half an hour or so, and then we are going on from there.'

'Would it not be easier for you to go directly to the restaurant and meet him there?'

'That is exactly what I suggested, but Tim said he would really like me with him. He is being rather mysterious. He won't tell me what it is all about. I gave up trying to get it out of him eventually I just told myself that boys will be boys, and we women have to indulge them from time to time,' she said with a shrug.

'He never gave you a hint, even?'

'No. Completely close mouthed. Men can be so infuriating at times! However, I suppose the great mystery will turn out to be that the brewers are introducing a new lager, and the honour of unveiling it upon an unsuspecting world has been bestowed on Tim, and he – simple soul that he is – will be over the moon! Either that or something similar, no doubt.'

'You are probably right. But I can hardly wait for morning to find out.' Veronica laughed.

'Got to love you and leave you, or I'll be late, and that would never do. Elizabeth donned her raincoat, waved good night and swallowed the last of her coffee.

When she had gone, Veronica's eyes wandered around the shop. She could hardly believe that a month had passed since opening day. Time had simply flown.

Phillip and Tim had come for the big day, and brought a bottle of champagne to celebrate the momentous occasion. Both girls had been delighted that the boys had disrupted their own busy lives to lend their support.

Veronica especially had been very surprised that Phillip had made the effort to come, what with the new job and his moving into his cottage – it really was a special courtesy on his part.

Trade had proved to be far better than hoped for, and Phillip and Tim had been pressed into lending a hand over the lunch period, when a coachload of tourists stopped in the village, and poured into the shop all at once. It had been hectic for a time, but great fun and very profitable too. The boys had said they enjoyed it immensely, and had volunteered to help out any time.

She remembered the conversation that followed.

'Phillip, you haven't told the girls where your first assignment is,' said Tim. 'Come on, I'm sure that they are waiting with baited breath to hear your news.'

'You've received your first assignment, and you've not said anything yet? Is it a state secret?' Elizabeth had asked, smiling broadly.

'No, it is certainly nothing secret, Elizabeth. I just thought because this is a very special day for you both, I didn't want to detract from your moment.'

'You and Tim have been wonderful, Phillip, how could you possibly detract from that? And, we are both dying to know where you are going,' Veronica had said.

'I believe you. I am going to Siberia!'

'Come on, be serious. Siberia indeed,' Elizabeth had scolded.

'I am totally serious. I am being sent to Siberia for my first assignment.'

'You really are not kidding us! They're sending you to Siberia? What on earth are they sending you there for? There is nothing but snow and ice there!' Veronica had protested.

'Siberia is thawing out quickly at this time of the year. I am assured that it is actually quite pleasant, in fact. The area boasts over a million lakes, and countless rivers. Ideal fishing, as they are virtually untouched by man. The producer was fortunate enough to have been invited there last year, and he had a wonderful fortnight. Best fishing of his life, he swears.'

'Sounds as though you should have a nice time. Do you stay in hotels?' Elizabeth asked.

'Now you are kidding – hotels, in the middle of Siberia?' Phillip had laughed. 'No. I am afraid that we shall have to stay in tents. I am rather looking forward to it – it should be quite an experience.'

'Tell them who your guest celebrities are, Phillip. Wait for it, ladies, you won't believe this!' Tim had sounded envious.

'You never mentioned that you would be having guest stars on the show, Phillip. The way that Tim is acting, it must be someone very famous, surely,' Veronica had said.

'Well, I have three different guests for the shows. The producer books them – I have no say in the matter at the moment. I hope to change that if the show succeeds.'

'Come on. Stop hedging, tell the girls who you will be staying in a tent with!' Tim had said mischievously.

'This is becoming more interesting by the second, Veronica. He must have a Hollywood beauty lined up for the sleeping bag!' Elizabeth had chided.

'Okay. You win, I'll tell you. We are doing three shows out there, and naturally we have three guests lined up. For the first show, Ivan Ustinov, the Russian cosmonaut, is the guest. The second is someone you may be more familiar with, Simon Steele. You know, the actor. I am not too sure if you'll know the third.' He had paused deliberately, removing a notebook from his inside jacket pocket. 'Ahh yes,' he'd said as he looked in the book. 'Someone called Barbara – I think she is some sort of film star.' He had been looking as innocent as a new-born lamb.

'The Boobs! You have the Boobs on your show! You think she is a film star! The most famous cleavage in Hollywood!' Elizabeth had said in amazement.

'I would not say "cleavage", Elizabeth. I think Silicone Valley would be a better description!' Veronica had interjected sarcastically.

'You are right, Veronica! I forgot that she is supposed to have had implants.' Elizabeth had laughed at her friend's wit.

'Methinks I sense a little of the green god of jealously, Phillip,' Tim had observed, enjoying every moment of his friend's obvious dilemma.

'I won't be there alone with her. The producer and the director, two cameramen and a sound man, not to mention the Russian officials who will be there as well, will be with us all the time, plus I forgot to mention her husband, Stuart Whiteman, and he is a lot bigger than me!'

'You mean you really do have Barbara Winssom as a guest? We thought you were having us on. Honestly, Phillip,' Veronica had said, pleading innocence, 'I mean, what could she possibly know or even care about fishing?'

'I am told that she has a degree in botany, and has been angling since she was a young girl. She is expert at tying flies, and is going to demonstrate her skills on the show. She is also a recognised expert on the medicinal plants that are native to the locality, and she is going to point them out on camera and describe their uses. I am also assured that she is a very nice person as well.'

'I guess that puts us in our place, Elizabeth. We were only having fun, Phillip. We certainly did not mean to offend you, and I apologise if we did,' Veronica had said sincerely.

'No offence taken. I thought that you were both serious –I didn't know how to react. I am sorry. I guess I am not used to girls with a sense of humour.'

'You must be tremendously excited at the prospect of meeting all these famous people. I know I would be shaking in my shoes. I am not sure if I could handle it,' Elizabeth had said.

'Believe me, I am not too sure myself. In truth, I am shaking in my shoes. I only hope that I don't dry up when the time comes to actually ask them questions in front of the camera. And I hope and pray that the fish are obliging, and I am not kidding. Imagine being in the middle of Siberia and filming an angling programme, and the fish not biting. It's a nightmare that haunts me!' Phillip had said with real passion in his voice.

'I am positive that you most certainly won't dry in front of the camera. I have never known you to be silent for more than ten minutes in your entire life!' Tim had said confidently. 'And when the fish realise that Barbara Winssom is there in person, they will be queuing up to get caught.' They had all laughed heartily.

'When do you leave, Phillip?' Veronica had asked him.

'I leave later tonight.' This had taken both the girls by complete surprise.

'Oh Phillip. Here we are teasing you, and you have been so kind in coming here today when you must have a thousand things you should probably be doing instead. I feel guilty, and very grateful too. It really is very nice of you. Thank you,' Veronica had said.

'It is my pleasure being here – I wouldn't have missed it for the world. I honestly don't mind the teasing. I guess that I'll have to get used to it if I am going to be around,' he'd said with a huge grin on his face.

'Sorry to break up the mutual admiration society,' Tim had remarked, 'nut we will have to be leaving, Phillip, otherwise you'll miss your flight.'

'When do you return?'

'I should be home in four weeks, but I am going straight to Ireland on my return, so it will actually be closer to six weeks that I'll be away, I guess.'

They'd had a glass of wine, and then the men had left for Newcastle airport in Tim's Mercedes. Phillip had to meet the producer and the director there, and then fly on to London. Their flight to Moscow was departing Heathrow in the early morning. Veronica had felt her heart sink a little as she watched the car disappear from view, secretly wondering if indeed she would ever see the handsome Phillip again. Why should a man who was deemed to mix with the rich and famous from now on, have any desire to come and visit a plain old Jane like her? She loved him madly, but she knew within herself that the best that she could hope for was a strictly platonic friendship.

She came back to the present with a start. No sense dwelling on what she knew could never be. Phillip would never be hers; she was resigned to that now.

The shop premises were an old blacksmith's forge and stables, which had held four horses in their heyday. Veronica had been given the building by her mother, who two years ago had met a very nice man when she was staying in Florida for the winter. They had had a whirlwind romance, and got married within six weeks.

As her mother had been widowed for twelve years, the thought that one day she might remarry had never crossed Veronica's mind, and to say she had been stunned by the phone call from Miami breaking the good news, was the understatement of the year.

A few weeks later the happy couple had arrived in England to allow her mother to attend to her affairs. Veronica liked her new stepfather immediately. He was tall, with dark hair going thin on top, brown eyes and a nose which had been broken at some time or another – an old football injury, he had explained – square-jawed with a powerful neck supported by huge shoulders. He was broad-chested with a narrow waist. All in all, a very athletic figure of a man in his late fifties.

Veronica's mother, now the new Mrs John Vialli, had explained that he worked out every day, and possessed his own gymnasium. A private fitness coach visited three times a week, no less. John was of Italian extraction, with English, French, German and even Apache Indian blood in his background. Like most Americans, he was a little obsessed with his roots, her mother had confided.

He was a Real Estate broker, and had done extremely well for himself, accumulating enough to retire to Florida and live comfortably by his early fifties. A widower for five years, falling in love had been as big a shock for him as it had been for her mother.

John proved to possess a great sense of humour, and had kept Veronica in stitches during their visit. Between his good looks and sense of fun, she could readily see why her mother had fallen for him.

The day prior to their leaving for Florida, her mother had handed the deeds to the house and the old smithy to her.

She explained that she wanted to be satisfied that her eldest daughter would always have a roof over her head.

Veronica had protested. She had said that her mother was forgetting that she also had another daughter, and that she could not possibly accept the title deeds to the properties, as surely her younger sister Melanie was entitled to half.

'Don't you worry yourself on Melanie's behalf. I have already given her fair share in cash when she came over for the wedding,' her mother had said with satisfied smugness.

'Melanie was at your wedding?' Veronica could not believe her ears. 'How could she possibly have been at your wedding when you told me yourself that you informed no one that you were marrying?'

'You know how it is, Veronica. I simply had to have someone of my own with me. So, naturally, I sent for Melanie. Somehow, it never even occurred to me that you would like to be there. Well, you just don't have the personality to fit in at a large formal occasion. Do you, my dear?'

Tears welled in Veronica's eyes as she thought back to that moment. She couldn't blame her sister. Her mother had probably told Melanie that her boring old sister was far happier staying in England, and didn't want to come.

The sad part was that her mother couldn't understand why Veronica was so hurt and even angry at her.

'You are the strange one at times, Veronica,' she had told her.

Veronica had been livid, and had told her mother in no uncertain terms that she would tell John exactly what she thought of him as well, when he returned from the pub.

Poor John, it transpired, was blameless. Her mother had confided (Veronica thought it more of a confession) that she had told him a little white lie, saying that Veronica was unable to attend their wedding as she had exams. John had been very understanding, and it was he who had insisted they visit England at the first opportunity to meet her.

When John returned a short time later, the loving mother-daughter relationship seemed intact, and Veronica had gritted her teeth and maintained the pretence until their departure. She could not bring herself to spoil John's holiday by quarrelling with her mother – she respected him too much – and so mother triumphed again.

Her thoughts turned to Elizabeth, and what she had said before leaving that evening. Veronica was equally curious as to what possible reason Tim might have in asking Elizabeth to meet him at his solicitors. She could not imagine what it could be that he felt it necessary to have Elizabeth along. She could only surmise that he wanted her to give him moral support.?

Men are strange creatures at times, she mused.

The shop door opened, letting in a cold blast of air, immediately snapping Veronica from her reverie. Turning to face the doorway, she gave an involuntary gasp. Two figures clad in black leather were standing there, wearing black crash-helmets fitted with black visors pulled down over their faces. She almost died of fright. Her heart was racing, and she desperately wished that she had not been so magnanimous in agreeing to Elizabeth leaving early.

One of the figures raised a hand and pulled the visor up – and there stood Cindy Crawford!

'Cindy! You scared the living daylights out of me! I thought you were going to rob me or something.'

'I am sorry, Veronica. I only meant to surprise you, not give you a heart attack,' Cindy said apologetically.

'That's alright. I just got a fright. It is good to see you,' Veronica replied with a smile, having regained her equilibrium. The person with Cindy was in the process of removing their helmet, and Veronica couldn't believe her eyes. It was Phillip! But he was supposed to be in Ireland.

'What on earth are you doing here, Philli …' she stopped: he looked like Phillip, yet it wasn't Phillip. A younger version of him stood there, smiling the exact same smile.

Cindy stepped in: 'Veronica, me old mate. Meet Greg. He looks a lot like Phillip, eh? He is his cousin, actually. Greg, meet Veronica. How's the shop doing then? I bet you are quiet with this terrible weather.' All this was said in a single breath as usual.

'Very nice to meet you, Greg. Cindy – how are you?' Veronica gave Cindy a great big welcoming hug. 'I must confess, Greg, that for a moment I thought you were Phillip. The resemblance is remarkable.' She could feel her face turning pink with embarrassment.

He must have heard her calling him Phillip.

'I am pleased to meet you, Veronica. I have heard a lot about you … Please don't feel embarrassed. If one managed the impossible and got a word in occasionally when Cindy is around, I would have introduced myself sooner. But with motor-mouth here, if I get in one word an hour, I feel pleased with myself,' Greg said with a huge grin on his face.

'Very amusing, Greg Marden. You know you are the strong silent type, which forces me to compensate and talk for the both of us,' Cindy countered. 'I reckoned that as Phillip only had eyes for you, Veronica, I had better grab this one for myself when he showed up at the hotel looking for Phillip. The poor blodger didn't know what hit him! Did you, my pet?' she said, patting his behind, and giving him a huge kiss on the cheek.

'You'll never change, Cindy Crawford,' said Veronica. 'How do you put up with her, Greg? You must have the patience of Job.'

'I told you, Veronica. He didn't know what hit him back at the hotel. He isn't demonstrating patience – he's still stunned! Anyway, where is Elizabeth? Her day off?'

'No, she's gone to meet Tim in Harrogate. I believe they are having a meal there. She'll be back in the morning. Are you planning on staying for a while? You are welcome to stay with me. That is my house on the left, Cindy. I have plenty of spare room.'

'Thanks, Veronica. We'd love to stay. Give Greg the keys and he can fetch in the luggage, and we can have a rare old natter. Come on, Greg ... wakey wakey! Get the keys and do your manly thing and carry in the luggage. Men do have their uses at times,' she commented, giving Veronica a wink.

'We phoned the hotel this afternoon to invite you over, but they told us you had left. Where have you and Greg been? Touring about on that motorbike, no doubt.'

'Yes. Greg took me to Perth in Scotland, and then we just toured the Highlands a bit, but the weather was terrible, so we gave up and came back down here. The scenery may be quite different, but the weather is exactly the same. Don't you guys ever get fed up with rain? I find it very depressing, I'm afraid.It can get a bit wearing, but we are more or less resigned to it. The good weather will be back.' Veronica tried to sound optimistic.

'My dad sent me much-needed funds when I told him I was doing my waitress thing. Male pride. "No daughter of mine is being reduced to a servant!" he said indignantly. Of course I knew he would react that way,' Cindy said, grinning widely. 'He sent money the same day. I was about to leave when Greg showed up looking for Phillip, and the rest is history.'

The shop door opened; Greg entered and handed Veronica the house keys.

'The kettle is in the back shop apparently, Greg. Be a love and make a pot of tea,' Cindy said, blowing him a kiss.

'What did your last servant die of?' Greg asked.

'Thirst! So look out, fella!' She beamed at him, 'My old man will love him,' she said to Veronica.

'Are you going to Australia with Cindy?' she asked Greg.

'No. My old man will be over here soon enough when he discovers the truth,' Cindy said mysteriously.

'What do you mean by the truth?'

'Didn't I tell you? When we were in Scotland, we visited Gretna Green. It seemed such a pity to waste the journey we thought, so we got married!'

Chapter Four

Veronica stood transfixed: she simply couldn't believe her ears. 'I get it. You are having me on! A joke is a joke, Cindy, but don't you think you are taking this one too far? Marriage is something too serious to joke about.'

'Cindy has her own rather unique way of putting things, but she wasn't joking, Veronica – we really are married. We didn't just jump in as nonchalantly as Cindy puts it – we are in love, and we both, and I emphasise both, discussed the matter very seriously indeed before we made the decision to marry, It wasn't a spur of the moment thing, despite the impression my wife gave you. Cindy darling, you really must learn when humour can give people the wrong impression and can backfire on you.' Greg stepped from the back shop and kissed Cindy lightly on her cheek.

'You really are married? I can't believe it! You cannot have known each other for any more than a month at most. Are you really not kidding me?'

'Come on, Veronica. I am sorry for being so flippant about it, honestly. We do know what we are doing, and I'll prove we are married,' Cindy said as she removed her leather motorbike gloves, and held out her left hand to Veronica. A brand new gold wedding band graced the third finger of the outstretched hand.

'You really are married! Wow! I've never known anyone who got married at Gretna Green. How romantic.

Congratulations!' She kissed the bride and groom. 'May your lives be filled with happiness.'

'Thanks, Veronica. I thought for a moment there that you were going to come on strong as though you were our guardian!' Cindy said with an expression of relief on her face.

'You only have yourself to blame, Cindy. I honestly thought you were playing a joke on me. I am truly very happy for you both. You are obviously meant for each other – it is as clear as daylight to me now. You obviously love each other. Oh, wait until Elizabeth finds out, she'll be green with envy. She and Tim are quite a hot item, you know. How romantic! I still cannot believe you were married at Gretna Green – it's the stuff that romantic novels thrive on. When did you get married?'

'Yesterday. Three forty-five pm to be precise,' Greg replied, grinning widely.

'Yesterday! You can't have told many people then?' Veronica said.

'No. You are the first to know, actually,' Cindy said.

'When we pluck up some courage, we'll get around to telling our families, and won't that be fun!'

'I certainly don't envy you. How do you think your parents will react, Greg?'

'They'll hit the roof at first, but my mum is pretty understanding, and she'll soon talk dad round. He will huff and puff a lot, but he is harmless really. And I know he will love Cindy, so that is half the battle won already.'

'What about your parents, Cindy?'

'I have only my dad to face. I think he might go off like an atomic bomb, to be honest, but eventually he'll see things my way. It could take a while. He can be so obstinate at times.'

'Sorry. I forgot you had only your dad. l do hope he understands, and is not too awkward. How long can you stay here? A few days at least, I hope.'

'Gee. Thanks, Veronica. That would be great. Give us a little time to get our act together, so to speak. Just think, Greg – we'll be able to tell our grandchildren that we honeymooned in the English

Lake District. 'Boy – you are certainly looking ahead, Cindy. Your grandchildren, no less! Mind you, it is a lovely thought,' Veronica said wistfully.

'Which is the lovely thought, the grandchildren or the honeymoon in the Lake District?' Greg asked, looking at both women with interest.

'You keep asking stupid questions, and the only thought you'll be having is how cold it is sleeping on the back of a motorbike in the rain,' Cindy said to her husband, giving Veronica a knowing wink.

The shop door opened and two ladies entered and began to browse, admiring various pieces as they progressed along the length of the wall. They kept giving Greg and Cindy nervous glances and then Greg remembered that they were still wearing the motorbike leathers. No wonder the women were giving them funny looks, he thought, and he suggested to Cindy that they go to the house and get into more comfortable clothes.

The ladies seemed to relax immediately the two leather-clad riders departed the premises, and much to Veronica's delight, they asked her many questions about the artists and potters whose wares she stocked, and spent a considerable sum of money before leaving. A few minutes later, one of them returned and bought the hand-carved pipe that Veronica had been fooling with earlier in the day when she was mimicking Sherlock Holmes for Elizabeth's amusement. 'I know I shouldn't really spend any more, but my brother will love this pipe, and I just have to have it,' she confided.

Dinner! The thought suddenly struck her as the customer left with her purchase. She must do something special. After all, it was not every day that a friend dropped in to announce that she had just got married. What to do? She had a few supplies in the freezer, but nothing adequate for making a. special meal. There was a small hotel in the village, but she was not too sure what time they stopped serving meals. She looked up the phone number and dialled, hoping against hope that they served dinner until at least ten o'clock. She was bitterly disappointed when the girl on the other end of the line told her they stopped serving dinner at eight. She looked at her watch: it was already seven thirty, much to her surprise.

The door opened and Cindy came in, dressed in jeans and a sweater. 'Do you fancy going for a bite to eat when you close up?' She asked Veronica.

'I am just off the phone to the inn, but they told me that they stop serving meals at eight o'clock. I'm afraid that we'll just have to settle for pot luck. I am not too sure what is in the fridge, but I am sure we can rustle up something.' she said with a smile, trying hard to hide her disappointment.

'No worries. We came prepared. We are treating you, Veronica. Mind you, it will be home made, but Greg is a wonderful cook, and I am not just saying that because I just had the good sense to marry him.'

'I can't have you doing your own cooking on your honeymoon, Cindy!' Veronica protested. 'You tell Greg that I'll prepare a meal when I close the shop.'

'Don't be silly. Greg really enjoys a stint in the kitchen, honeymoon or not. Too late anyhow – he's started already. He sent me over here out of his way, actually. Takes his cooking very seriously! A real romantic honeymoon to tell the kids about someday. Huh? He was too busy cooking in the kitchen to cook something up with me, I'll be able to tell the old man. That ought to pacify him.'

'You'll never change!' Veronica said as she cashed up for the day, laughing all the while. 'Does that poor man realise what he has taken on? How on earth will he manage to stay relatively sane married to you? You take nothing seriously. I envy you, Cindy. I wish I could be like that. Elizabeth is always telling me that I take life too seriously.'

'Sometimes I wish that I could keep my big mouth shut and at least give the impression that I can be serious about some issues, but I have the uncanny knack of putting my foot in it every time, without fail,' Cindy replied truthfully. 'So you see, it doesn't always pay to have a sense of humour, you know.'

The meal that Greg had prepared took Veronica completely by surprise. He was a wonderful cook. Chilled melon slice provided the starter, followed by chicken liver pate with very thin crisp pieces of lightly toasted bread. The main course was saddle of lamb cutlets, flamed in a brandy cream sauce served with baby roast potatoes and sliced green beans, fried in rich butter with just a hint of garlic. It was delicious. Sweet was a pineapple and passion fruit cheesecake. Veronica had never tasted this before, and she simply adored it.

'That was one of the finest meals I have ever eaten, Greg. You are to be congratulated. When Cindy said that you were good in the kitchen, I had no idea just how good. That was a meal that any top chef would have been proud to have been credited with. It was utterly fabulous. Where on earth did you learn to cook like that?'

'Just a hobby. I find cooking very relaxing. I am glad you enjoyed it, Veronica. Just our way of saying thanks.'

'You have nothing to thank me for. There will always be room for you both here. What are friends for? One thing I must know. When did you get time to buy this food? I am astounded that you managed to purchase the fresh fruit here.'

'I bought it when you two were having your gossip earlier. The fruiterer across the street had it all on display, so there was no problem.'

'I can't believe it. That shows how observant I am of things on my own doorstep! I never realised that Mr Smythe stocked exotic fruit. But then, I have been rather preoccupied with the opening of the shop this long while.'

Greg laughed. 'I think you are slightly out of touch, Veronica. Passion fruit and fresh pineapple are not considered exotic fruits these days. As a matter of fact, they are almost considered mundane. They are available in every supermarket in the country, and I imagine every fruit shop as well.'

'Cooking has never been my strong point. I guess that is rather obvious.' She blushed. 'Nevertheless, I may not be much of a cook, but I do know when I have eaten an extremely good meal, and I assure you that I just have. Thank you again, Greg.'

'You are most welcome, Veronica, and it was a pleasure to prepare it.'

'Hmm. If you two are quite finished with the mutual admiration society bit, how about a glass of champagne, Greg? By the way, sport – you have convinced me. You have my permission to feel free to cook breakfast in the morning,' Cindy said, blowing her new husband a kiss.

'I have an even better idea, Cindy. You, by your own admission, are not too hot in the kitchen. So why don't you get in some practice and make breakfast? I am sure Veronica would appreciate it, being served breakfast in bed before having to get up for work. I know that I am looking forward to it already, darling. My mouth is watering already,' he said, licking his lips with mock relish.

'If you don't mind burnt toast and fried eggs that resemble rubber in texture, then you are on! I'll make brekkie,' Cindy replied with a smile.

'I think you both should have a nice long lie-in in the morning,' said Veronica, raising her hand as both guests made to protest. 'I will make breakfast, no argument about it. That's settled, then. What do you do for a living, Greg? Oh, I am sorry. That was terribly rude of me.'

'Think nothing of it, Veronica. I have been very fortunate. I have just signed with Yorkshire to play cricket this season. I'm really excited about it. I only hope that I am good enough over the season to make the grade. My most cherished dream has always been to be able to be a professional cricketer. This is my big chance. I hope I don't blow it!'

'I am sure that you will prove a great success. With Cindy's support I am positive that you can only go from strength to strength,' Veronica said, encouragingly.

'He'll be too frightened to do otherwise. Won't you, old sport? If he messes around on the field, he'll soon discover that I can throw a few googlies better than any bowler he has ever faced! Cricket is my second name. I was raised by a cricket fanatic. That is our saving grace, I think actually, Veronica. My old man is a cricket nut, and when he calms down long enough to listen, the fact that he has a cricketer for a son-in-law just might swing things in our favour. So you'll score a century when I talk him into coming to see you play, won't you my darling?' Cindy gave Greg a playful sock on the chin. 'That is, if you know what is good for you,' she added, smiling broadly, obviously very proud of him and the fact that he had been selected to play for Yorkshire.

'With Greg tied here for the year, that means that you won't be returning to Australia to finish your degree?' Veronica asked Cindy.

'Nope. I'll wait and see what happens. Kidding aside, if Greg makes it then we are looking at a whole new ballgame next year. We'll play it by ear, and just see what happens. I may be able to go to uni here. I don't know yet.

My dad will have more than enough to say about it. I have decided to be diplomatic and let Greg and him sort it out between them. You know, man to man and all that stuff. Then I'll do whatever I decide myself!' she said with a mischievous smile.

The next morning, the newlyweds were fast asleep when Veronica looked in to see what they would like for breakfast. She had not the heart to waken them, so she left the Teasmade filled with water at their bedside, and crept out of the house.

Veronica opened the shop, and of course put the kettle on as usual. She put coffee in both mugs, and put biscuits on a plate. Elizabeth was normally twenty minutes late in the mornings. Rising from her slumbers was not her strong point. Veronica had become accustomed to this, and she had developed a routine, allowing for her partner's slow start. The kettle came on the boil, and she made the coffee without giving it a thought. Elizabeth should be coming through the door just as she was putting the mugs on the tray.

Two hours later, Elizabeth still had not put in an appearance, and Veronica began to worry a little. This was not like her. She was usually late, but never as late as this. Her mobile seemed to be switched off.

She decided to phone Elizabeth's mum and see if she had been in contact with her. She did not really want to phone, but something told her she should. Elizabeth would not be too pleased with her, but she felt that it was time to act. Mrs Leeson hated being bothered at home – she did not approve of Elizabeth investing in the shop, and had made it very plain that she wanted nothing to do with it.

Veronica replaced the receiver, her ear still ringing from the outrage that Elizabeth's mother took upon herself to feel at being disturbed at her elevenses with such a stupid question. She pointed out rather forcefully that Veronica, was her daughter's partner, and therefore it was up to her to know where she was. If they insisted in playing at shops, then they should at least be competent enough to know each other's whereabouts during working hours, and if not, then it was high time that they were stopping all this shop nonsense and doing something more befitting their circumstance … and then she hung up the phone with these words of wisdom.

'Ooh! That woman. I swear that she has the mothering instincts of a cuckoo!' Veronica said aloud.

'Who has the instincts of a cuckoo?' Cindy asked.

'I never heard you come in, Cindy. I was on the phone with Elizabeth's mother. I'm afraid that I was referring to her. No one was supposed to hear me, but she has the knack of infuriating one so. Elizabeth has not come in to work today, and I phoned to see if Mrs Leeson had heard from her. I am sorry now that I did. All I got for my trouble was a tirade on how Elizabeth and I should be doing something more befitting us as ladies. A rather moot point with the said lady, I am sorry to say.'

'Have you phoned Tim to see if he knows where she is?' Cindy asked.

'No. I didn't want to disturb him at work. He is very busy in the mornings preparing the meals for the lunches. I am rather worried, though – it just isn't like Elizabeth to be so late without even phoning. I think I'll have to call and see if he knows what has happened.' Although she was unwilling to disturb Tim, she was beginning to feel that she no longer had any choice in the matter.

A few minutes later, she replaced the phone, and turned to Cindy, wearing an extremely worried frown. 'That was Tim's solicitor. Tim is not at work either. His solicitor says that Tim and Elizabeth will be in contact with me as soon as possible. He said he was not at liberty to divulge anything else, whatever that is supposed to mean. He divulged absolutely nothing to me, except to tell me that Elizabeth won't be in today. It is all very mysterious.'

'Oh no! Perhaps they have run off to Gretna Green as well. Wouldn't that be a turn-up for the books!' Cindy said, smiling broadly at Veronica.

'Really, Cindy. You do have an extraordinary imagination at times. Gretna Green indeed! Lightning only strikes twice in novels, not in real life. I just wish she would phone me and let me know what is going on. I am her business partner, after all.'

'I wouldn't worry too much. If there was something wrong with Elizabeth, surely that lawyer would have told you. He couldn't keep something like that from you – it wouldn't be ethical. Elizabeth will be in touch soon. I feel it in my bones, and my bones are never wrong, I'll have you know.'

'I am sure you are right, Cindy. It is just so unlike her, that's what I find disturbing. I guess she and Tim will phone me when they can. Where is Greg, by the way? Surely you have not had a tiff?'

'Of course not. He'd be too scared to pick a fight in case I said I was going back to Australia!'

'Oh Cindy – you wouldn't threaten to do that, surely?' Veronica asked, feeling slightly shocked by the idea.

'I was only joking, Veronica. Don't take everything so literally. You'll enjoy life more that way, believe me. Greg is out doing grocery shopping, actually, and he prefers to do that alone. He says that I have as much idea about food as he does about the mating habits of the kangaroo.'

'You certainly have a way with words, you two. Why don't you put the kettle on and we'll have a cup of coffee? I must finish wrapping this ornament – the customer will be here to collect it shortly.'

'Sure thing. By the way. I couldn't help noticing the photo on your mantelpiece. The girl in it looks a lot like you. Who is she?'

'Do you really think she looks like me? Most people cannot see any resemblance. Her name is Melanie, my younger sister.'

'She looks familiar. I suppose it is because she looks like you. But somehow I seem to have met her before, yet I know I haven't. A strange feeling.'

'She is an actress. She has appeared in a few films, and quite a lot of television programmes. Could be you've seen her on TV or at the cinema. She is not a star yet, but I have no doubt that she will be before too long. She always succeeds in anything she tries. I believe she is not a bad actress, actually. To tell you the truth, I have not actually seen her act myself, but Elizabeth says that she is really quite good. So I suppose she must be then ...' Veronica tailed off.

'I get the distinct feeling that Melanie is not exactly flavour-of-the-month with you, Veronica. What is it, a slight touch of jealousy? No,' Cindy answered her own question. 'You are far too nice to be jealous of anyone. I bet she thinks you are a fool too, same as Elizabeth's mum does, for having the shop when you could be out in the world chasing a rich husband.'

'How on earth did you know that?' Veronica replied in astonishment. 'I haven't even told Elizabeth that Melanie had said that to me. In fact she actually thinks I have a screw loose – her exact words. She cannot see why anyone could possibly want to work the hours we do. She says it just isn't natural. I am amazed, Cindy. You are very intuitive at times.'

'I have definitely seen her on TV, and believe me, in certain roles she isn't acting so much as recreating parts that are very familiar to her in real life, I'll bet. I can tell these things. She doesn't have to act the bitch – it comes naturally, I guess. Am I right or am I right? That is how I guessed what she had said to upset you. Easy really.' Cindy was very matter of fact about it.

'I doubt if Melanie would be too pleased with your impression of her, but I must say I think it's pretty accurate, actually. She really is a nice girl, just a little over-ambitious at times in my estimation. I guess that just because we are sisters does not necessarily mean that we have to think alike. Melanie and I certainly never have, not even as children. I guess we never will.'

'Takes all kinds to make a world, and there would be no fun in life if we all thought the same, now would there?

Mind you, it must be a wee bit exciting at times to have a movie star, well not star exactly, but you know what I mean, as a sister. Glamour and all that – it certainly must be a talking point at parties. Has she brought any big stars home to meet you?'

'No. Melanie only drops in occasionally, and I doubt very much if she would want any of her show-business friends to know that she has a sister who runs a shop. Not up-market enough for her circle, I am afraid.' Veronica had the trace of a smile playing on her lips.

'Too bad she's not got your nature, Veronica. She would have been a star long ago if she had. Maybe I'll get the pleasure of meeting her someday, and then I can judge her for myself. I wonder where Greg has managed to get to. I thought he would have been back by now. I mean, how long does it take to fetch a few groceries, for Pete's sake?'

'Just long enough for a husband to take the time to buy his wife a dozen red roses, that's all,' Greg replied as he entered the shop laden with the flowers and two bags of groceries.

'You are a romantic fool, Greg. But I love you for it. Please promise that you won't change when we get older.' Cindy cupped his face in her hands and looked lovingly into his eyes.

'I promise,' Greg said as he put his packages on the floor, and then handed Cindy the roses. 'Now, how about a cup of coffee for a hard-working man?'

'Certainly, my darling,' Cindy replied as she sampled the fragrance of the roses. 'Elizabeth has not arrived for work. A bit of a mystery, really – Tim has not appeared at his pub either. I was just saying to Veronica that they have probably gone to Gretna Green. Won't they be surprised when they get back and discover that we beat them to it?'

'That would be funny,' said Greg, 'but I don't think Tim is the sort that would do anything as rash as that. He isn't a romantic like me. He is the "think before you leap" type. You have no idea where they could be, Veronica? Didn't Elizabeth give you any kind of clue yesterday?'

'No. I wish she had. I am at a loss. I simply cannot for the life of me think where they can be, or what they can be doing. It is so unlike Elizabeth, but Tim's lawyer is at the pub, and he doesn't seem to be concerned. All he would tell me is that Tim and Elizabeth will contact me as soon as possible. All highly mysterious indeed.'

'I know. Perhaps Tim is really a spy, and they are on their way to a safe house,' suggested Cindy. 'Probably down in Brazil. Spies always go to Brazil. He looks a little like James Bond, so I guess that that settles that, he is a spy for sure!'

'Cindy, you have a greater imagination than Ian Fleming himself. Spy indeed! Your idea that they have eloped to Gretna Green is more plausible. Come to think of it though, Tim does look a lot like James Bond,' said Veronica, nodding her head in agreement.

'I told you. Mind you, the one big difference between Tim and James Bond is, that while Bond is licensed to kill, Tim is licensed to spill.'

'Licensed to spill?' said Veronica and Greg at the same time.

'Yes. To spill drinks, of course!' Cindy said with a grin.

A coach stopped, unleashing a horde of very welcome tourists, and Cindy and Greg pitched in, helping Veronica cope with the onslaught as best they could. It was a very hectic forty minutes, and extremely welcome and much-needed business.

'Thank goodness for coaches. When the weather is as bad as this, we would starve without them,' said Veronica. 'And thank you very much for your help – I just don't know how I would have managed without you.'

'No sweat, Veronica. Be a doll and put the kettle on, Greg. Wow – now there is a familiar sight! Well, perhaps a tiny bit over the top, wouldn't you say, Veronica?' said Cindy, with a mischievous glint in her eye.

Veronica looked out from the shop window, and there was Phillip's bright red Cadillac parked at the door. Her heart leapt for joy. He was already walking round to the passenger door, which he held open. He obviously had someone with him. Long silk-stockinged legs started to emerge from the vehicle. They seemed to be endless. Phillip moved to the side to allow the mysterious lady to gain the pavement. Veronica's heart sank to the soles of her feet. Standing there, smiling sweetly at Phillip, was the last person she expected to see. It was her sister, Melanie.

Chapter Five

The following morning, Veronica sat staring at the rain running down the window of the shop, many thoughts racing through her head, all of them depressing. She heaved a big sigh, generally feeling very sorry for herself. Phillip had left for his home shortly after they had eaten the dinner Greg had prepared. He had, of course, only cooked enough for three but had worked miracles, and in no time had magically produced a veritable feast satisfying everyone's hunger. He was a treasure indeed, she mused. Cindy had really landed lucky.

Once the news of the Gretna Green wedding was absorbed, and advice had been freely given to the happy couple by both Phillip and Melanie. The subject had then turned to the mystery of the whereabouts of the itinerant Elizabeth and Tim. Phillip had not heard from Tim for a few days. They normally kept in touch by phone, but Tim had not answered for about four days, Phillip reckoned.

He had not been too perturbed by this, as Tim had a habit of forgetting to charge the battery of his mobile.

Veronica had asked if Phillip could think of any reason for Tim not to want his whereabouts to be known and he'd laughed at the very idea of such a thing.

'Tim is the most open person I know,' he'd said. 'There simply is no rational explanation I can think of. I suggest that we give them until lunchtime tomorrow, and if they have not contacted one of us, then perhaps Cindy would be so kind as to look after the shop for a little while in the afternoon, and you and I will go and pin that lawyer down to explain exactly what is going on, as it's obvious that Tim has confided in him.'

Everyone had agreed to this, and the talk had then come around to Phillip and Melanie. Phillip had told how he had been recording a programme in Ireland, and a film crew were shooting a movie nearby, and some of the cast were staying in the same hotel. Melanie was, of course, in the cast, and they had met in the bar the night he had arrived. Now it so happened that one of Phillip's guest stars had gone down with flu. The director had been talking quite a bit to Melanie – he had in fact taken quite a shine to her – and he persuaded the producer to book her as a replacement for the ailing star. After a few drinks on the director, the poor man had given in, and

Phillip was given the task of trying to make Melanie look like an expert angler in the course of one day. The Irish gillie who had been hired for the duration of filming proved to be worth more than his weight in gold, Phillip had said. He had taught Melanie to cast a fly, and he had even gone to the length of catching a salmon and keeping it in a tank in case they could not get a fish to bite during filming, the idea being that he would attach the unfortunate salmon to Melanie's line, just to make her look good for the camera. After all, he said, a girl as beautiful as Melanie could not be seen failing to catch a fish now, could she? Fortunately, a rather large salmon duly obliged the morning of filming, and the gillie's "safety net" had not been required.

'Your sister has the luck of the Irish, Veronica,' he'd said. 'I have been fishing all my days, and to tell the truth, I have never actually caught a salmon, try as I may. She goes out for half an hour, and catches a twenty-four pounder! Wouldn't it make you want to weep?' Phillip had smiled at Melanie, who'd smugly replied that some people have it, and some don't.

'Much to my surprise,' he had continued, 'my father arrived at the hotel the last day of the shoot. He was in the area inspecting some property that was on the market, and was awaiting the Sultan's arrival in the morning, having decided that the property was worth investing in. Dad was disappointed that I would be on my way home before the Sultan arrived at the hotel, so he invited me to come down to the estate for a few days before I have to resume work. Melanie was in the bar with me at the time, and naturally she was included in the invitation. We'll be heading down tomorrow, as soon as the mystery of Tim and Elizabeth has resolved itself.'

'Tell Veronica how you found out that we are sisters, Phillip,' Melanie had said. 'It was fate, really – Phillip and I were destined to be together. You'll see.' She had given a satisfied smirk.

Veronica had known at that moment that her sister sensed she had feelings for Phillip, and was going to take every opportunity to rub it in that she, Melanie, had him, and would keep him until such time he no longer suited her purpose.

'Quite extraordinary, really,' Phillip had said. 'I just happened to mention that I was coming here to see how you and Elizabeth were, and how the shop was doing. Melanie heard the name of the village, and immediately asked if by any chance I was talking about Veronica Shillingworth? When I said yes, she started laughing, saying "how extraordinary", I was talking about her sister! Difficult to believe, but the truth, all the same. Naturally, we decided to come together.' He'd beamed at Melanie, and Veronica's heart had ached a little more.

Now she sat staring absentmindedly at the rain pouring down the window. Common sense told her that she could never compete with Melanie, but Melanie could most certainly compete with the glamorous guests that Phillip was likely to encounter during his career. She knew in herself that having Phillip was never anything but fantasy, but losing him to Melanie was a cruel blow indeed. Fate could be so unkind.

The ring of the telephone gave her a start, bringing her back to reality with a jolt. Sheer relief gave way to joy, and then anger as she heard Elizabeth's voice on the other end of the line.

'Where on earth are you? You have had us all worried stiff, Elizabeth. You could at least have phoned me.'

'I am sorry, Veronica, honestly. But I have not had a chance to phone. We'll be home about ten in the evening. Explain everything then. Bye' and at that the phone went dead. Veronica didn't know whether to jump for joy, or burst a blood vessel in anger. She was still wrestling with her emotions when Cindy came in twenty minutes later.

'What's up sport? You look as though you have the cares of the world on your shoulders. Come on, it can't be as bad as that, surely?' Cindy said, trying to get Veronica to smile.

'I just had a phone call from Elizabeth. She said that they will arrive here at about ten o'clock this evening. That was all she said. No explanation as to where they have been. I am really verging on exploding when she appears. I hate losing my temper at any time, but I'm fighting very hard to control myself right at this moment, I can tell you, Cindy. I really am at a total loss as to what Elizabeth and Tim are playing at.'

'I bet you they have a perfectly plausible explanation when they do arrive, and you will be the first to console or congratulate them, whatever the situation calls for.

'You are probably right, Cindy. I suppose I am better letting off steam now. Less chance then of saying something I may regret later. I am sorry to be such a moaning Minnie. You must consider me to be a real pain!'

'Don't be silly, it is perfectly natural for you to worry. I still say that Elizabeth will come in through that door and announce that she and Tim got married at Gretna Green,' Cindy said, noticing with satisfaction the smile appear on Veronica's face.

'You really are totally incorrigible, Cindy Crawford.'

'Less of the Crawford. I'll remind you that I am Mrs Marden now.' She feigned hurt feelings.

'Oh. I totally forgot. I do apologise, Mrs Marden!'

'We'll forgive you this time. Any more slip ups though and I shall be forced to take serious action and inform your sister that you are head over heels in love with Phillip. That will sort you out.'

'Cindy! Don't you dare say a thing like that! Not even in jest. I never said that I am in love with Phillip. Melanie would take you seriously, and do her utmost to keep Phillip away from here. I like him as a friend too much for that, so please don't kid around when Melanie is within earshot. Please!'

'My dear Veronica, I did not mean to upset you so. I am sorry. But I'm afraid that any fool can see that you are hopelessly in love with Phillip. Probably even Melanie,' she said in a kindly tone, trying to pacify her friend.

'Am I as obvious as all that? Do you really mean that I completely fail to hide my feelings? I am so embarrassed – I don't know what to say.'

'Why be embarrassed? Loving someone is a perfectly normal and natural thing. Give Phillip time. Some men are pathetically slow when it comes to realising that they are in love. He probably thinks that Melanie is the bees' knees right now, but he'll soon realise that beauty is more than skin deep, you'll see.'

'The wise old sage has spoken!' Veronica said, smiling sweetly at Cindy.

'I know that I have just reminded you that I am now a married woman, but that does not necessitate the prefix "old", I'll have you know. Wise, most certainly. Old? Forget it!' She laughed.

Veronica looked at Cindy and then said: 'I must admit that for a little while last night I thought that Melanie was going to have the nerve to invite Phillip to stay with her – under my own roof! I can tell you, Cindy, I gave a great sigh of relief when Phillip insisted that he had to go to his own cottage to see to his mail etcetera.'

'Phillip is a gentleman. He would never do anything to embarrass you, Veronica. I wonder what Elizabeth and Tim have been up to? Nice and juicy goings on, I reckon,' she said with a wicked grin spreading over her face.

'You are terrible. Poor Elizabeth has probably been as innocent as a new-born lamb. Well, perhaps the lamb's mother!' Veronica said, winking.

Phillip duly arrived at the shop a little before one o'clock, and was very pleased to learn that Elizabeth had been in contact with Veronica. A few customers came in and browsed for a while, eventually purchasing one or two trinkets, but nothing to set the till alight. Still, Veronica commented, every penny counted in the kind of weather like they had been experiencing. A customer with a pound to spend was a very welcome person indeed.

The day passed slowly, with business just as slow as well, Veronica commented to Cindy, and they both laughed, albeit half-heartedly.

Tim and Elizabeth arrived shortly after ten as promised. Everyone stood in awkward silence for a moment, and then Elizabeth said: 'I ... that is we, rather ... are very sorry if we have caused you any anxiety. It was entirely unintentional, believe me.'

'What happened? It is so unlike you not to be in touch at least, Elizabeth. I'm so relieved to see you. I, or rather we, have been worried sick wondering if you were okay, or if you had been taken ill or worse.' Veronica had poured it all out before she realised it. She really did not want to vent her anger on Elizabeth: reason told her that her partner must have had a perfectly good reason for her absence.

'Please. I think that I had better do the talking,' said Tim. 'After all, it is my fault that Elizabeth has not been in contact until this morning, Veronica. Now, why don't we all find a seat, and I'll do my best to explain.'

'Before you start, Tim – could I possibly ask you to put the kettle on, Veronica?' said Elizabeth. 'I am dying for a coffee. Cindy immediately popped into the kitchen and filled the kettle, then asked everyone if they wanted coffee or tea. Veronica thanked Cindy, and then asked Tim to continue.

'I got a request from my solicitor in Harrogate last week to attend a meeting with him three days ago. He also suggested that I bring Elizabeth with me, but would not give me a reason for this request over the phone, which l must admit annoyed me no end at the time. Do you remember my uncle George, on my father's side of the family, Phillip?' 'Yes, I do.'

'Well, it transpired that he passed away a month ago. He and my dad never really saw eye to eye, and in fact they had hardly spoken in years, actually. They did not exactly ignore one another, just tolerated each other and no more. Dad could never accept that his only brother was gay. He never even tried to accept George for what he was. "Sick" was the only term I ever heard dad refer to George as, and as long as he chose to pursue his lifestyle, then he was no brother of his! Dad was adamant on that point.'

Cindy came into the living room and served the coffee.

Tim and Elizabeth accepted theirs gratefully, both thirsty after their journey.

'I, on the other hand, always liked George, and his sexual preferences did not bother me. Of course, he never married, and in fact spent the last thirty years in San Francisco. He said that he had the freedom to do and live as he wished there I was really sad to hear of his death – as I said, I always liked him.' He paused to take a sip of coffee.

'George could not have been very old, Tim,' said Phillip.

'No, Phillip, but he had AIDS. He must have known he had it when he was here last, but said nothing to anyone. He was a very private person, and indeed that was the way he preferred to remain until the end. He moved into a private nursing home in California, and that is where he remained till he died. He left strict instructions that no one was to be contacted, not even when he died. He had his cremation all arranged, and his instructions were carried out to the letter. My solicitor received their instructions from a firm of lawyers in California long after his funeral had taken place, if you could call it a funeral, that is. He had his ashes scattered in the Pacific Ocean. No service, no mourners. He said that he always hated funerals, and did not wish to impose his own on anyone. A very private man, or a very private eccentric, depending on one's point of view, I suppose.'

'I guess if he lived in California for thirty years, people probably considered it to be quite rational behaviour to request no one attend his funeral. Strange place, California,' Phillip observed. 'Well, as I have already told you, my Uncle George never married, therefore had no direct heir. To my utter amazement, I was told that he had left the bulk of his estate to me! He stated in a letter placed with his lawyer that I was the only member of the family who took him at face value, and treated him like an ordinary human being, and not a leper. This still astonishes me. I only treated him as I found him, and that was as a very warm person, and I never understood why dad took the attitude he did. After all, George was his brother.' He paused for a sip of coffee, and then he lit a cigar. 'Sorry for smoking in the house, Veronica, but my nerves are still shattered after the last few days.'

'I'll forgive you this time, Tim.' She smiled a comforting smile.

'I knew that George had a few business interests, but I did not know what in. I don't think my dad knew either, actually. My solicitor read George's will to me and I was, to say the least, utterly flabbergasted. He left some sums of money to certain charities in the States, and left my dad a quarter of a million dollars. He bequeathed me the rest of his estate, with a proviso that I will explain to you later. He left me all his business interests, plus houses in San Francisco, New York, and Kingston, Jamaica. Also an apartment in Cannes, and a motor yacht he kept at Catalina Island in California. It is capable of sailing to Hawaii non-stop from Catalina apparently. He also left me ten million dollars in cash. Now comes the proviso, and the explanation as to where we have been the last few days, Veronica.' Everyone sat in silence, enthralled.

Tim took a long pull on his cigar. 'I think it better to tell you what George's business was. He was in the hotel business. I never knew that. He had not one, but a chain of no fewer than seventeen hotels in the States, and three in the Caribbean. He also had interests in shipping and airline companies and – this is the icing on the cake – he owned a beauty parlour for men in San Francisco! Fortunately, he bequeathed that to a friend! The one other thing he left me is the one that had the proviso attached. He left me a television studio that was his pride and joy, seemingly. The thing that makes it a wee bit different is that its programming is directed at and for the gay population. The proviso is that I must run it personally, and ensure that the policies he set when he first started the station will be continued. He said that I am a fair man, if he is any judge of character, and he entrusted me to carry on with his work even though I am in his own words, "straight". I am not allowed to sell the station as long as it makes a profit, and I cannot change the name. It is called – my dad will love this – the Jones-Belling Gay Time TV Channel. I think it's a riot. He probably called it that just to annoy my father!' Tim laughed heartily.

'This is all quite astounding, Tim, and I am delighted for you. But it still does not explain why you and Elizabeth have not even been in touch,' Veronica said, beginning to feel rather peeved.

'I am coming to that, Veronica. I had to explain about the will so you'll understand why we did what we did. The other stipulation was that I have to live in America, in order to run the TV station personally, and I had to give the solicitor an immediate answer. By immediate, I mean I had one hour, believe it or not. George said in the will that if I required more time, then I was not the man he thought I was, and the deal would be off. Elizabeth and I went for a coffee, and we reached a decision together. We know how we feel about each other, so it was an easy decision in the end. We told the solicitor the answer was yes, and then the ball started rolling at the speed of light. He asked if we had passports. Of course we both possess them. He rushed us home to collect them, and then we were taken to London and put on a flight to Washington. We were met there by lawyers from California, and put on a private jet and flown on to San Francisco. The papers were signed before the day was ended, and George's estate was mine. It was all so fast, I still can't believe it!'

Cindy replenished the coffee, and everyone waited with baited breath for Tim to continue.

'Wow! This is better than a Hollywood movie,' Cindy whispered to Veronica.

'I happened to mention to Hank, that's the lawyer in San Francisco, what our plans were. He told me to leave it to him and before we knew it, we were on our way to the airport, and on a plane and heading for Las Vegas. One thing you have got to hand the Americans, they certainly don't hang about! When we arrived in Vegas, we were met at the airport by a chauffeur and a huge stretch limousine. It was like a bus! We were whisked off to a hotel, had a meal ... Hank was with us all the time, by the way. Then we were back in the limo, and driven to a justice of the peace, and before we knew what had hit us, we were saying "I do!"'

Everyone in the room exchanged puzzled looks, then Cindy suddenly yelled out: 'Am I psychic, or am I not? I told you they would come back married, Veronica!'

All eyes in the room stared at Cindy in bewilderment, then suddenly they all spoke at once.

'You are married?' they all said in unison.

Tim and Elizabeth joined hands, and embraced. Then Elizabeth held out her left hand, exposing the wedding ring adorning her finger. Veronica rushed to hug her partner and lifelong friend.

'I am so happy for you both. Congratulations!' she said, tears of joy streaming down her cheeks, as she gave Elizabeth a kiss.

Pandemonium reigned for a while, as everyone tried to congratulate the couple at one and the same time. Slowly, order was restored. and an impromptu party to celebrate both happy couples' weddings got underway. A great time was had by all. Veronica was still partying when she discovered that it was breakfast time, and she would have to open the shop without having had the luxury of any sleep.

The others continued with the celebrations a little longer before at last succumbing to sleep. Veronica, poor soul, had no option but open the shop on time. Weariness hit quite suddenly, and she had to keep a regular supply of coffee close to hand. A few customers came in during the morning, which helped her keep her attention on business, and not straying into a romantic fantasy in which she and

Phillip ran away to Niagara Falls to get married. A fantasy indeed, she mused .

Suddenly, she was wide awake as a thought struck her with the force of a sledge hammer Elizabeth would be living in America from now on! What was going to happen to the shop? Veronica had invested everything she possessed in the venture. Elizabeth had invested twenty thousand pounds in cash. What if she wanted it returned?

What on earth was she going to do if Elizabeth insisted on pulling her money out? She had already mortgaged the house to raise the money to carry out the building work that had to be done to bring the smithy up to scratch and convert it into the shop, and the bank had advanced her a ten-thousand-pound overdraft facility, which was sitting dangerously close to its limit. Her heart pounded with anxiety as she pondered her dilemma. The shop door opened, and much to Veronica's surprise, Elizabeth stood in front of her looking as bright as a button.

'I thought you would be asleep for hours yet. Surely you must be exhausted after the travelling you have just done?' Veronica said.

'I know, I should be. But I feel fine, honestly. I had to come over and see you as soon as I could. Tim is still sleeping like a baby. I am sorry if you were worried about me, Veronica, but I just simply did not have the opportunity to phone you. Everything happened so fast!' Elizabeth sounded sincere.

'Don't give it another thought, Elizabeth. I understand perfectly now, and I am so thrilled for you!'

'Thanks, Veronica. I still can't believe it – it all happened so fast! I do love Tim so, and I know we shall be perfectly happy. How have you been? Apart from worried, that is.'

'Oh, I am fine thank you, and it has been really nice having Cindy and Greg here. What a surprise when they turned up and said that they were married! I honestly thought that they were kidding me. I just hope that they don't put off telling their parents the good news for too long, though.'

'They've not told their parents yet? Wow! The longer they postpone it, the harder it will become. I do hope they are going to be sensible and tell them soon.'

'I know this is a rather awkward question at this time, but have you given any thought to what you want to do with your share in the business, Elizabeth?' Veronica asked, feeling slightly embarrassed at having to pose the question.

'As a matter of fact, I was just about to broach the subject myself, Veronica. Tim and I discussed it on the flight back over here. I know that you cannot afford to buy me out, and to tell you the truth, I would rather like to keep my investment in the shop – if it is alright with you, that is?'

'Yes. I was hoping you would say that. I have been a little bit concerned. I know that you will be living in the States from now on, and I really was not too sure if you would want to retain your interest being so far away. What a relief! I just couldn't imagine where I was going to get the cash to buy your share.' She was visibly relieved.

'Good. Just one other point, Veronica. You have your house on mortgage to secure your end of the finance. Tim and I feel that this is more than a little unfair on you. We have plenty of money now, and we would like to pay off the mortgage, leaving the business in a stronger financial footing. We would still be fifty-fifty partners, and the savings on mortgage payments will compensate you for my absence. Obviously you cannot be expected to be here all on your own – you will have to employ someone. Think it over. I am sure you'll agree that is a sound idea.'

'I don't know what to say, Elizabeth. I couldn't possibly allow you to pay off my mortgage. It is far too much money,' she protested.

'Don't be silly. We can well afford it, and after all, you are the one who is being left to cope. Tim and I insist that you accept. You thoroughly deserve to have the strain of day-to-day financial pressures lifted. Please say yes.'

'I don't know how I shall ever be able to thank you and Tim. I accept, and I promise that the shop will be one of the best gift shops in the country before I am through!' She gave Elizabeth a great big hug.

'Good – I am so pleased. Have you any idea who you can get to help out?'

'Well … Cindy will be here in the area for at least this season. Greg is going to be playing cricket for Yorkshire this year. Perhaps she may be interested. I'll ask her. She would be a great asset, I am sure. She has such a lovely personality, and the customers love her. She has given me a hand a couple of times since she arrived. I think it might just suit her at least for the season, Elizabeth. Oh, I am so happy for you. I do hope that you will like living in America – San Francisco looks a lovely place when you see it on television.'

'I am sure l will like it. We were taken to see the house there – it is simply out of this world. Veronica, I want you to come over at the end of the season. I am sure that you will love it too, when you see it. Let's make that a firm date. You are coming over at the end of the season, and no excuses! Shake on it,' Elizabeth said, extending her hand, and grinning like a Cheshire cat at her friend.

'I would love to come. It is a date, then,' Veronica replied, shaking Elizabeth by the hand.

'What's Tim going to do with the pub? You haven't had a lot of time to reach a decision, really. What a rush for you both.'

'He is meeting his accountant and solicitor later today, along with the brewery. We'll just have to wait and see. Then we are going to tell my mother our news. I haven't had the courage to tell her yet. When she learns that Tim has money, he'll be the greatest thing since sliced bread in her eyes, I have no doubt. You know her, Veronica – the whiff of cash, and she will be over the moon. When she finally realises just how much he is worth, there will be no living with her. She will be unbearably snobbish and arrogant. I don't envy you being left here. When she deems fit to lower herself to come in to the shop, you know as well as I that it will only be to gloat.' She shook her head. 'Why are parents like that? I hope and pray that I will never be when I have a family, Veronica. I swear that I won't.'

'I am positive that you won't be. You and I have had to live with false snobbishness since we were children. Our mothers are two of a kind.' She sighed. 'By the way, I phoned your mum to see if she had heard from you. I am sorry, but you know I would only do such a thing as a last resort. All I got for my trouble was a lambasting because I didn't know where you were. Incompetent, I think she called me.'

'I won't even apologise for her Veronica. You know her as well as I do. I doubt if either of us would expect anything else, really?'

'If the shoe was on the other foot, and you were phoning my mother, you would most certainly have got the same reaction. You know it, and unfortunately, so do I,' Veronica replied with a shrug of the shoulders.

Suddenly, they burst into peals of laughter. 'How many times have we had this same conversation over the years? I don't suppose either of them will ever change.'

The shop door opened very quietly, and Elizabeth almost jumped out of her skin when a loud female voice suddenly demanded: 'And where exactly have you been, young lady?' Standing before her, looking none too pleased, was her mother.

Chapter Six

'Thank you, please call again,' Veronica said in a courteous manner as she held the door open for a lady who had just purchased a large piece of pottery. The lady smiled and thanked her for her service and the time she had taken showing her the range of pottery she carried in stock, and explaining the intricacies of manufacture involved in making a large piece such as her purchase. She promised to pay the shop a return visit the next time she was in the vicinity. Veronica felt rather satisfied with herself for once – she was quite convinced that the lady would indeed keep her promise and return. This was what it was all about, building a rapport with one's customers, and converting them from just casual shoppers into cherished clients.

Elizabeth had phoned Tim from the shop when her mother arrived so unexpectedly, and then they had gone with Mrs Leeson to let her know their happy news. Veronica did not envy either of them one little bit – Elizabeth's mother could be very difficult at times, and one could only guess at her reaction to her daughter's elopement. The money would undoubtedly help pacify her though, once her initial outrage was over.

'Hi, Veronica,' said Cindy as she entered the shop. 'Thanks for last night – it was simply wonderful. We all had a great time. Well, you'll be pleased to learn that we have decided to take the bull by the horns, and go and see Greg's folks to tell them the good news, they have just gained the world's finest daughter-in-law!'

'I don't think you should phrase it that way, at least not for the first five minutes,' Greg said as he followed her into the shop.

'Look at it this way, my dear, they are better finding everything

69

out at once – that way there are no surprises in store for them later. After all, don't you think that they have just gained the best ever daughter-in-law that any parents ever had?' She winked at Veronica and then added: 'I'll put the kettle on while he thinks about it.'

'When are you going to see your parents, Greg?' Veronica asked.

'We are going to go this afternoon, just in case we lose our bottle if we wait a day or so. Better get it over with. I phoned home and they will be there tonight. I didn't tell them why I am going down, and I never got asked, actually. They will be assuming that I am going to tell them about Yorkshire Cricket Club. Are they in for a slight surprise!'

'You can say that again. I only hope that your mother doesn't have a heart attack, but they are bound to love Cindy – she is such a lovely girl, with a personality to match. I have no fear that she will have them eating out of her hands before the day is out, and the only condemnation you will get is why you took so long to introduce her. She has a way with her, and she will win them over before you know it, Greg. So don't be too apprehensive.'

'Can we come back after we have done the necessary? I would really appreciate it if we could. I have to report for training in a couple of days' time and it would be rather nice for Cindy to be with someone she knows at first, until we get organised.'

'Of course you can. As a matter of fact, l was going to suggest it myself. I actually have a proposition for you. Cindy, how is the coffee coming along?' she asked, popping her head into the back shop.

'Ready,' Cindy replied, entering, carrying a tray with the mugs. 'Brought the chocolate biscuits that were on the shelf. Hope you don't mind?'

'No, that is what they are for. Please take a seat for two minutes. I have something I want to discuss with you.'

'Oh-oh! Sounds ominous. Got the bike ready for a quick getaway, Greg? She has twigged that you have nicked the family silver.'

'Be serious for a moment, Cindy. I want to ask you something. As you know, Elizabeth is going off to live in America, and that leaves me on my own to run the shop. We were wondering if you would like to work here for the season? Greg is going to be based here for the next few months at least, and I would love to have you here. You are welcome to stay with me, I have plenty of room, and to tell the truth, it would be rather nice to have some company for a change. You can commute to the cricket ground from here quite easily, Greg. What do you say?'

Veronica looked at them appealingly.

'Wow! What a beaut' of an idea! Thanks, Veronica. We'll take you up on your offer,' Cindy gushed.

'Hmm ... Don't I have a say in this?' her husband asked.

'Naturally,darling. As long as it is yes, feel free to say whatever your little heart desires.' She smiled and planted a kiss on his cheek.

'You win,' said Greg. 'Thank you, Veronica – we will be delighted to accept your offer. At least if I do make the grade, it gives us a chance to look at houses at our leisure, and gives Cindy company, as well as a job. Mind you, aren't you running a terrible risk employing this wild colonial? You can never be too sure what she will say next. She might just frighten your customers all away.' He winked conspiratorially at Veronica.

'I'll be frightening a certain husband away with a flea in his ear if he is not careful,' came the retort. 'Remember, I am about to get to know your mother, and then you are in trouble, my lad. You'll have two females to contend with then. Isn't life a real pain at times?' She giggled, and frisked his hair in a playful manner.

'Does Phillip know that you are going to see your parents, Greg?' Veronica asked.

'Yes. He was having a bite to eat when I phoned home. He thinks it the best idea I've had for a while. A bit sarcastic. Good job I know him or I could have been offended.'

'I'm sure Phillip did not mean to be sarcastic. He probably meant it was for the best that you contact them now instead of later. The longer you postpone a thing like that, the harder it becomes and the more hurt your parents would feel,' Veronica said in Phillip's defence.

'Wow – he must have impressed you, to jump to his defence so quickly. Remember, Phillip is my cousin, and we have been more or less brought up together. We are more like brothers, really, than cousins. We are sarcastic with each other all the time. Life just wouldn't be the same if we weren't.'

'I see. I'll remember that in future. When are you going to tell your dad, Cindy?'

'First things first. Like I said, we are grabbing the bull by the horns, and telling Greg's parents today, and then we are going to grab the same bull again, but this time by a more sensitive part of his anatomy, and phone my old man in Perth. That should be a lot of fun. You'll probably hear him up here, without the aid of a telephone, most likely. He has a bit of a temper, but he is a great guy once he calms down. I think I'll give Greg the pleasure of telling him that he is his new son-in-law! You'll enjoy that, won't you dear?' she said with a mischievous glint in her eye.

'Sometimes I am convinced that she married me for my life insurance, Veronica. From what she has told me about her father, he is likely to jump on the first plane over here, and beat me to a pulp for having the audacity to marry his little girl,' Greg said, smiling at his wife all the while.

'Relax. He won't jump on the next available plane over here, my darling. He will probably jump on his own plane and fly over here. He has his own private jet. Didn't I tell you? Sorry. It must have slipped my mind.' She watched the expression of alarm spread over Greg's face.

'His own jet? You are taking the old mickey out of me. Aren't you? He surely hasn't got his own jet? I mean, nobody but the Sultan and his crowd can afford to own a jet!' Greg replied, not entirely sure if Cindy was kidding or not.

'Yeah, honestly. He has his own jet. A Boeing 707, to be precise. Well, when I say it is his, it's a company plane, actually. But of course, he owns the company, so I guess it is his jet. What do you think, Veronica. Is it his own jet?'

'Is it a limited company?' Veronica asked.

'No. It's a private company. So I'm right, then? He does own his own jet?'

'I suppose he does – you should know the answer to that better than me, Cindy. You are the one training to be an lawyer, come to think of it.'

'I told you, I am only studying law to suit my dad. I don't really pay a lot of attention to the lecturers. I look upon them as part of the furniture. A necessary evil, if you like. I guess I forgot to tell you that he is also one of the wealthiest men in Oz, Greg, but don't let that bother you – it never has me!' she said, smiling like the cat with the cream.

'Come on, Cindy. You're kidding, aren't you?' Greg said. 'A man who is as wealthy as that would never let his only child wander all over the globe by herself. Fun's fun – but be serious for a moment for once in your life and tell me the truth. What does your dad do for a living?'

'I am telling you the truth, Greg. Have you never heard of Crawford Industries? They make everything under the sun. Have you heard of Ozzie Desert Quench?'

'Of course I have. That's the biggest selling lager in Australia – even I know that! It is sold here as well.'

'Have you ever read the label?'

'No. Can't say I have. Why?'

'Veronica, did I see some Ozzie Desert Quench in your house last night?'

'I believe you did, Cindy. Isn't that the beer that Phillip brought in with him?' Veronica replied.

'Greg, I want you to run over to the house and see if you can find a bottle. An empty one will do, as long as it has its label on. Will you be a dear and do that for me, please?'

Reluctantly, Greg consented and went to fetch the lager bottle.

'Are you kidding him, Cindy?' Veronica asked.

'No, honestly, Veronica. I guess this is one of those times when being a great kidder has backfired on me. If he finds the bottle. I'll prove to him what I am saying is true. I cannot for the life of me see what difference it makes whether my dad is rich or not. It's me that Greg married, not my old man!' she said with exasperation.

Greg returned, carrying a lager bottle as requested.

'Good. It still has its label. Now, darling, look here,' Cindy said, as she pointed to the small print on the bottom of the label. 'Please read out what it says.'

Greg took the bottle and studied the label. 'Made in Perth, Australia, by Crawford Industries.'

'Now take a close look at the girl in the photo behind the print,' she said. Greg studied the photo behind the bold print, and suddenly he gasped. 'Believe me now?' Cindy asked smugly.

'It's you! It really is you! I believe you! Look, Veronica, its Cindy on the bottle. Unreal! Wow! My wife's photo on lager bottles sold all over the world. Isn't that something? I'll probably end up wearing lager bottles when daddy dear finds out that we are married. 1 still can't believe it's you on the label,' he said as he admired her photo once again.

'You are a famous Cindy Crawford then. Holding out on us, were you?' Veronica jested.

'No, not really, Veronica. My name never appeared on the labels. I only posed for the photos to please dad. He is so proud of his little girl, it makes me want to scream at times. I agreed to the photos to suit his vanity, not mine,' Cindy said, trying very hard to convince them that she had no pretensions to fame.

'I believe you, Cindy,' said Veronica, laughing. 'Now, where did Phillip and Melanie get to? Did you see them before you came across to the shop by any chance?'

'Yes. Melanie was still in bed, and Phillip was crashed out on your sofa when I left. l guess they are probably still sleeping, it must have been very late when they arrived' Greg answered.

'I hope you are not using my name in vain,' said a voice from the doorway. They turned in unison to greet Phillip as he entered the shop.

'Well, well. Look what the cat dragged in,' Greg said mockingly.

'It would take a fair-sized cat to drag me in, kiddo. Are you going to see your parents today? I hope so,' Phillip said.

'Yes – we are leaving shortly. I am not exactly looking forward to it, but it must be done,' Greg replied glumly.

'A man's gotta do what a man's gotta do, old boy,' Phillip said. grinning at his cousin's discomfort.

'And a girl!' Cindy chipped in.

'I hope you are going to tell your dad too. The same thing applies. A girl's gotta do as well, you know,' Phillip answered, giving Veronica a knowing wink. 'I don't think big Tom would be too pleased to find out that you told Greg's folks and forgot to tell him.'

'How do you know his name is Tom?' Greg asked, looking very puzzled.

'Easy. I met him when I was down in Perth covering the Americas Cup,' Phillip answered.

'What is he like, Phillip? I can't really get a straight answer from Cindy. She has been trying her best to scare the daylights out of me, telling me he has a terrible temper. Almost uncontrollable in fact.'

'I suppose he is all right if you take him the right way. I got on fairly well with him. He is very forthright, and very surly too. He threatened to punch out a bloke's lights for him because he heard him say that the States were bound to win the yacht race. He really got uptight at that.'

'That's my dad alright,' Cindy said proudly.

'I wouldn't worry too much, Greg. If he decides to take a swing at you, you'll never know what hit you. He's built like King Kong! Just one word of warning. He dislikes … in fact I was told hates … Pommies. Thats Australian for Englishmen. Rather you than me, old son. It must be love indeed!' he said, and tousled Greg's hair as he went into the back shop, keeping a poker face.

'He makes him sound even more awesome than you do!' he said to his new wife, who was trying very hard not to laugh.

'Not to worry, lover. He wouldn't dare hit a husband of mine,' Cindy consoled. 'At least I don't think he would.'

'Don't you listen to them, Greg. They are worse than children. I am sure that Mr Crawford will be very reasonable once he gets over his initial shock. Anyhow, look on the bright side – you have your crash helmet for the bike, so he couldn't inflict a lot of damage if you put it on!' Veronica said.

'Thanks for the advice, Veronica. I'll make sure that I spend the rest of my life wearing my crash helmet,' Greg said with a hint of sarcasm.

'Sorry, . I didn't mean to make matters worse. I wasn't trying to make fun of you, honestly. I have an unfortunate habit of saying the wrong thing at the wrong time.'

'I am the one who should be sorry, Veronica. It is just that those two have been winding me up . But don't you worry. I'll get them back – wait and see. And just when they least expect it. Be warned you two, it is war!' he said, looking at Cindy and Phillip, and making the shape of a gun with his fingers. 'Bang! We will see who gets the laugh!'

'Good for you, Greg. I think you are going to have to learn to stick up for yourself a little more. You should be ashamed of yourself, Phillip Marden, winding poor Greg up like that,' Veronica scolded.

'Don't you go feeling sorry for him, Veronica. We have been winding each other up all our lives. It is a game we play. Greg knows that, and he enjoys it, despite his protests, which are aimed at gaining your sympathies, you know. Don't be fooled by that innocent cherubic face – he's winding you up right now, but you didn't twig. Come on – tell her, Greg.'

'I thought that Veronica understood that we always take the mickey out of each other. I am sorry – Cindy obviously knew that Phillip was taking delight in leading me on, and she joined in herself. I thought that you were taking part in the game too. Believe me, if Phillip thought that I was in any danger from Mr Crawford, he would be the first to come to my defence. On second thoughts, I sincerely hope that he doesn't have to!'

'Don't count on it!' Cindy interjected, pulling a face at Greg.

'Very funny! I'll probably end up getting along with your dad better than you do!'

'And then you had better watch out, smarty pants!'

'Are you going on that motorbike of yours?' Phillip asked Greg.

'Sure we are. Why?'

'It's just that I am leaving myself quite shortly, that is as soon as Melanie is ready, and it would seem sensible for us all to travel down in my car. I am coming back in three days' time, and you could come back with me. What do you think? The weather is not exactly conducive to riding a bike now, is it?'

'What do you think, Cindy – should we trust him to drive us two?' Greg asked his wife.

'Oh. I don't know, Greg. Do you think it would be safe enough? After all, he is getting on a bit, and the reflexes tend to slow down with age., do you think we should risk it?'

'What do you mean, I am getting on a bit?' Phillip said with mock hurt in his voice.

'I would have thought that that was rather self-explanatory. Have you ever looked at yourself in the mirror when you are shaving? You really should, you know, and you wouldn't have to ask such an idiotic question, old sport,' Greg said, a note of triumph in his voice.

'That was a masterstroke. I have to hand it to you, Greg – well done.' Phillip replied, smiling in admiration at his cousin.

'I told you I would repay you when you least expected it! Truce?'

'Truce,' Phillip replied, and they shook hands, both of them grinning like puppies with two tails.

'Men! I really don't think they ever grow up,' Veronica said to Cindy with a sigh of resignation.

'You have not answered my question. Are you coming in the car? It really makes sense in this weather.'

'Yes, we'd be delighted to. Thanks, Phillip. I didn't know you were taking Melanie with you,' Greg said.

'Didn't I say? She was in the hotel in Ireland having a drink with me when my dad came in. You know him and a pretty face! He immediately invited her to come with me for a few days. I could hardly say no, especially when Melanie had accepted the invitation with the speed of light. She told me later that she had overheard dad telling someone in the hotel that he was going to see the Sultan at the estate. I guess that the lure of a real live Sultan was too much for her to resist. She admitted to me that she made sure that she accepted dad's offer before either of us had the chance to refuse. Quite a girl, that sister of yours!' Phillip said to Veronica.

'You can say that again,' Veronica replied, feeling her heart sink again. Melanie was winning, as per usual.

'Are you two packed yet?' Phillip asked Greg and Cindy.

'Yes – we are all ready to leave as soon as you are.'

'Then we are just waiting on the delectable Melanie,' Phillip said, quite oblivious to having said anything out of place. Veronica's face visibly fell at the remark, but only Cindy noticed.

'You never told us how you got on in Russia with Barbara Winssom. Is she as well-proportioned as she looks in the movies?' Veronica asked Phillip, desperate to steer the subject away from Melanie. 'I got on really well with her, as a matter of fact. She is a very nice lady, and her husband is extremely nice too. She is an expert angler. She can tie a fly in no time flat, quite amazing to watch. She did it for the camera, just to prove that is was no fluke when she tied her own Devon Minnow when we started fishing.'

'Big deal! What we want to know is are they real, or are they made of silicone as the papers say?' Cindy blurted out, quite unabashed.

'You surely don't think that I just asked her if her breasts were real or not? What do you think she would have said? Here Phillip, take a look for yourself?'

'You never know your luck. If you don't ask, you don't get!' Greg remarked, smiling wickedly at Phillip.

Cindy thumped him on the shoulder, playfully. 'You be very careful what you say, sport,' she said. 'Remember, you are a married man now, with a wife to answer to!' She hit him another friendly thump on the shoulder, just to ensure that he had received the message loud and clear.

'Ouch! I get it! I wasn't leering at the thought of Barbara Winssom, I was simply wondering how she could never compare to you, my precious.'

Phillip burst out laughing. 'If you believe that, you'll believe anything, Cindy!'

'Stop making it worse, thank you, cousin!' Greg scolded, winking at Phillip, and mouthing 'You can tell me later.'

'I heard that, Greg. Careful,' Cindy chided, giving Veronica a great big smile. 'A jealous female is a terrible sight to behold, don't you think, Veronica?'

'Definitely. He is flirting with fire, if only he had the sense to realise it.'

'Did I tell you that she speaks Russian fluently?' said Phillip. 'I couldn't believe my ears at first. She switches from

English to Russian with consummate ease, and then into French. There was a French TV crew there at the same time as us doing a wildlife film, and Barbra could carry on a three-way conversation almost simultaneously. She did not hesitate between languages- instant translation. I reckoned her as some kind of genius, but her husband assured me that people from the Prairies, in both the States and Canada, can speak several languages, and switch from one to the other effortlessly. He told me that

Immigrants of many nationalities settled in the West, and the languages were handed down through the generations. The more they inter-married, the more languages were handed down, and still are to this day. What an advantage North Americans have, and they are quite unaware of it.'

'I hope you did not include the lecture in your programme!' Greg remarked.

'Sorry. You should know me by now, Greg. I have a habit of going on a bit at times – you should have stopped me. Sorry, girls. I didn't mean to lecture you.'

'Don't be silly, Phillip. I found it very interesting. I have to confess, Barbara Winssom sounds a very nice person indeed from what you have told us,' Veronica said, smiling sweetly at him. 'Do you think that the programme turned out well?'

'Funny you should ask that. It went out on the satellite last week, and it was such a hit in the States, the producer has asked Barbara – and Stuart Whiteman, her husband – to do a follow-up with me in Scotland later this year. They have agreed, and only the dates have to be finalised. Apparently, they thoroughly enjoyed themselves doing the programme in Russia, and they said to tell me that I make a great host. "A professional to the fingertips" were their exact words. I was gobsmacked, to say the least/ I was literally shaking in my boots all the time we were filming. I guess I must have disguised my feelings rather well.' He was trying to sound modest, but he was all too obviously bursting with pride, and justifiably so.

'We told you you're a natural, Phillip, before you left for Russia. The camera must like you. To have praise heaped upon you by two such experienced people is really something. You should be proud of yourself,' Veronica said, secretly feeling as proud as punch of him herself, but unable to share her true feelings in public.

'Give it a miss, Veronica, or you'll have him so egotistical, he won't manage to squeeze his head in through the door,' Greg contested jovially.

'Very funny, Greg,' said Phillip. 'Jealousy is a terrible affliction, you know – just because I have met Barbara Winssom and you haven't, your eyes are turning green with envy. I can tell when a man is jealous. And I'll have you know that my head is certainly no larger than Barbara Winssom's bust line, and you all know how minute that is!' He kept a poker face throughout.

'Phillip Marden! You are even worse than Greg. Can't you two ever leave the proportions of that lady's breasts out of your topic of conversation for more than two minutes? What would her husband say if he could hear you?' Veronica asked in all innocence.

'He would agree with us entirely. Film stars are very proud of their assets, and I surely do not have to remind you of Barbara's? Stuart Whiteman is as proud as a peacock of his wife's assets, and he is the first to tell you. They are more valuable than Fort Knox, he told me, and he was perfectly serious.'

'I think that is totally asinine! What a chauvinist he is!' Veronica said, the feminist in her coming to the fore... but she would be the first to deny such a thing if challenged.

'I guess Barbara Winssom is a chauvinist as well, then. She expounded the same thoughts to me a day later,' Phillip replied in triumph.

'American film stars! One cannot expect anything else, I suppose,' Veronica replied, convincing herself that was explanation enough to justify her argument.

'Speaking of film stars, I wonder what your sister is doing? She should have been over here twenty minutes ago. Be an angel and give her a buzz on the phone and find out if she is on her way.'

'Did I hear my name being mentioned?' Melanie demanded to know as she entered the premises unheard.

'Melanie! We were just about to send out a search party to look for you,' Phillip jested.

'No need, I am here. Hale and hearty, and dying to go! I am so looking forward to our time together, Phillip.' She looked directly at Veronica as she spoke.

Veronica cringed inwardly, but managed a smile with a great deal of effort. 'I do hope you have a good time, Melanie, and I sincerely hope that you and Cindy have a nice reception from your parents. Greg – I don't envy you, but it has to be faced. Good luck.' she said, and gave them both a kiss of encouragement.

'You take care of yourself, Veronica. And please don't worry about Melanie, I'll see to it that she will be well taken care of, in the manner that she deserves,' Phillip said cryptically as he left.

Chapter Seven

Veronica watched the Cadillac fade into the distance with a heavy heart. She knew it was foolish, but she just couldn't help feeling rather jealous of her sister, driving off, sitting in the front seat of the car, smiling sweetly at Phillip, and giving Veronica a rather smug look as they went. It was almost too much to bear, but that was life, she told herself sadly as the large vehicle disappeared from view.

Cindy and Greg were obviously quite nervous at the prospect of having to tell his parents of their marriage. Veronica felt for them, but they had to face up to their actions sooner or later. She felt that the hardest task was still ahead of them, informing Mr Crawford! Somehow, Veronica sensed that he would not be so easy to persuade as Greg's parents. From what Phillip had told her of them, they seemed to be quite rationally minded people, who – once they came to terms with their son's marriage – would soon accept the situation. Cindy would be bound to win them over, she thought. Who could resist that bubbling personality, after all?

A few customers came into the shop, and Veronica busied herself serving, and generally being as helpful as possible. A young couple, who had entered after the others, spent some time admiring the hand-carved pipes that a friend of Elizabeth's carved specially for them, on an exclusive basis. Elizabeth had met him at art school, and he had become very successful since starting his business.

Whether one actually smoked or not did not seem to matter. Customers who had purchased the pipes did so mainly because they fell in love with his carving. They were really quite beautiful, and Elizabeth herself had purchased one as a gift for Frank, her mother's new husband. He treasured it, her mum had told her in a rare letter (writing was never her mum's strong point).

After a lot of discussion, the couple decided to buy no fewer than three pipes, one for their respective fathers, and one for themselves. It transpired that none of them actually smoked, but all of them were pipe collectors! This was a new breed of customer to Veronica – she never even knew that there were such people as pipe collectors. One to take note of, she thought.

The afternoon seemed to drag. The weather had improved slightly, but even the sight of the all-too-elusive sun did not cheer Veronica. Everything was so quiet with everyone gone. Elizabeth and Tim had not returned yet, and she was afraid that perhaps they were having a hard time with Mrs Leeson. She could be extremely awkward when she wanted to. Veronica hoped Elizabeth had not fallen out with her mother, a not infrequent happening. The door opened and two elderly ladies entered the shop, and Veronica had her attention taken for almost an hour, culminating in the purchase of a postcard. She smiled to herself as the ladies left the premises. Can't win them all, she mused.

She put the kettle on when the little old ladies left. She needed a coffee – spending an hour going over her entire stock was hard thirsty work, and not surprisingly, she was feeling a wee bit peckish. Then she remembered that she not had any lunch – in the excitement of everyone leaving at the same time, she had forgotten to eat.

A sandwich liberally laced with thick creamy honey did the trick. Veronica loved honey, and at times she was really thankful for that. When she was feeling particularly tired, she always found that a sandwich spread with honey gave her the energy that she needed. Thank goodness for the honeybee, she thought.

The day dragged on. The odd customer broke the tedium for her now and then, but her mind always drifted to the sight of

Melanie going off in the car, smiling up at Phillip, and the look of satisfaction when she waved to Veronica. There was no doubt whatever in Veronica's mind: Melanie knew beyond question that her sister liked Phillip, liked him a lot, and she was just the girl to play him along, and make Veronica suffer in the process as she had done so many times in the past.

A few more tourists than had been seen for a while appeared in the village that day, lured out into the open by the sunshine. Veronica revelled in the sheer pleasure of serving people, and answering their questions. She even took delight in gift-wrapping some purchases, a task that normally she would pass over to Elizabeth as she had never really mastered the art for herself. She would have to learn now, like it or not, and that was a certainty.

Looking at the time, Veronica wondered where Phillip and his passengers would be now. Not too far from their destination, she figured. She heaved a sigh, wishing that it were her sitting in that familiar big American car, instead of her sister. 'You really must get a grip on yourself, Veronica. This will simply not do!' she said out loud, scolding herself severely.

'What's this? Are you being a naughty girl, then?' Veronica looked up in surprise. She had been so engrossed in her thoughts that she had not heard Elizabeth and Tim coming in.

'I am sorry. I never heard you. Too wrapped up in my own thoughts, I am ashamed to say. How did it go with your mother? I am almost afraid to ask that.'

'She was a little surprised at first, to say the least. When she heard about Tim's inheritance, it was a different story then, I'll tell you, Veronica. He is the greatest thing since sliced bread, now. By the time we left, I was beginning to think that she found Tim for me herself! Unreal, my mother! Sliced bread here thinks she is wonderful. Don't you, my pet?' Elizabeth smiled at her husband, and tickled him under his chin. 'Mummy's little darling, aren't we?' she said.

'I really don't know why you two think that she is such an ogre. I take people as I find them. And I found your mother absolutely charming, Elizabeth. Sorry, but that's the way the cookie crumbles,' he said, shrugging his shoulders.

'Let's just say that we have known her a little longer, and have a slightly deeper insight into her personality. You should have told her that you had gone bust! You just may have seen her in a different light, then. However, I think it might actually prove to be a good thing, Elizabeth, if you think about it. She won't make a great deal of fuss when you leave for the States, and better an ally than an enemy. So be glad for small mercies.' Veronica put her finger to Elizabeth's forehead 'Use your loaf,' she suggested.

'You are correct, of course. I was only teasing Tim. It would have been an utter catastrophe if they had not hit it off. I am so relieved, actually, that I feel like celebrating.

Why don't we go to Harrogate for dinner and a quiet drink? What do you say, Veronica?' Elizabeth asked.

'I would love to, but I never got to bed last night, and I am really tired. Sorry. You and Tim go by all means – I won't mind, honestly.'

'I forgot that you have not had any sleep! Tim, be a darling and go to the hotel across the road and ask them to prepare something special for a takeaway dinner for three. You turn on the charm and I am sure that they will do it for you. They are still in the dark ages, and feel that their guests should be in bed by nine o'clock. Seriously! Be a dear and try your best,' his wife pleaded, looking lovingly into his eyes.

'I am as good as there, already. I'll procure us a dinner fit for a king, my darling. Trust me!' he replied with total confidence, and immediately made his exit, and headed straight for the hotel.

'He doesn't know what he is up against,' Veronica said.

'He'll soon find out. Bet you a fiver that he returns with at scrumptious meal. He will talk them into selling the hotel if he has to. One thing I have learned in the last few days is that Tim never takes no for an answer.'

'Greg returned empty handed, and Cindy thought the same as you – that he would persuade them to serve him just because he was charming and handsome – but it didn't work. You're on. A fiver it is!' Veronica said, her troubles forgotten as she removed a five pound note from her wallet and put it on the countertop. 'Put your money where your mouth is, or forever be silent!' she challenged.

Elizabeth responded in kind, and they laughed heartily. It had been a long day for both of them, and the strain visibly lifted with their laughter.

Twenty minutes later, Tim returned as predicted.

Veronica lifted the two five pound notes and placed them in her purse. 'I told you so, Elizabeth. The hotel owner is one of the most disobliging people I have ever met. He seems to think that the tourist are here strictly for his benefit, and that he is doing them a favour staying open till eight o'clock at night. He simply refuses to move with the times. Unfortunately, he does the village no favours with his attitude. The man should never be in the tourist industry. He simply has no idea of what it is all about.'

'I could not agree more, Veronica,' said Tim. 'He is the most stubborn person that I have ever met. I swear that I shall do my utmost to rectify the situation as soon as I possibly can. It was the attitude that he displays that gave this country a bad name for lack of service for so long in the international tourist business. I thought that had all been changed for the better – I was wrong. I am absolutely livid! What parochial thinking. It is almost beyond belief! He refused point blank to allow the waitress to serve me – can you believe that?'

'I believe you. Greg got the same treatment. How the hotel manages to stay in business I simply don't know.'

'Ah well. Never mind. I am sure we can think of something after you have cashed up for the night,' Tim said reassuringly.

'Funny you should say that. I just happen to have a gorgeous chicken curry in my freezer that Greg cooked,' said Veronica. 'He is a fabulous chef, Elizabeth. You won't believe how good his cooking is until you taste it. You two pop over to the house, and get it from the freezer and pop it into the micro. I'll be over in a jiffy.'

Elizabeth needed no persuasion – she was utterly famished – and Tim was hustled across to the house before he had the opportunity to protest.

'You certainly were not exaggerating when you said that Greg was a marvellous chef. That was the finest chicken curry I have ever tasted, Veronica – it was simply wonderful. I wonder where he learned to cook. Do you know if he studied cooking at all, Tim?'

'I don't think so, darling. He must just have a natural bent for it, I guess. I knew he enjoyed cooking, but I have never had the opportunity to taste his endeavours before tonight. I agree, it was sensational. If he fails the grade as a first-class cricketer, he will certainly succeed as a chef. I would guarantee him a job any time.'

'Praise indeed for the young man. A good job he isn't here. His head would be too swollen to make it through the door and Cindy would have a remark or two to make as well, I guess, just to keep him in check,' Veronica said, smiling broadly.

'We managed to pop into the bank today, believe it or not, and everything has been taken care of,' said Tim. 'Mr Stuart will drop into the shop tomorrow to see you, Veronica. He knows you are alone for the next few days and won't be able to go and see him, so he is bringing the necessary papers with him for you to sign. You'll have your house back free and clear once more, the way it should be. I thought he was going to kiss me at one stage when he realised the financial muscle I command! Elizabeth thought his performance was really funny. Didn't you, my darling?'

'No wonder,' said Elizabeth. 'He was almost doing cartwheels, it was like watching a performing seal, Veronica. You would have loved to have seen him today – if Tim had suggested that he jump through hoops, he would have done so without question. Great what money can do?' Elizabeth said, laughing ironically 'All I can say is thank you. You don't know what a relief it will be not having to worry about the mortgage, Tim. I imagine that Mr Stuart will have a slightly more friendly approach when he comes tomorrow. He has not exactly been very friendly or supportive recently. You would think that the bad weather we have been having was all my fault. "Remember your mortgage payments have to be kept up to date, Miss Shillingworth. The bank is not a charity institution, you know". That has been his battle cry for the last few weeks, making me quite nervous, actually.'

'You never mentioned it, Veronica,' said Elizabeth.

'I did not want to worry you. I knew that it was basically an empty threat. I think that man takes a delight in having power over people. It is something I have never been able to quite understand why some people are like that. I dare say, though, that he makes an ideal bank manager, from the bank's point of view. He certainly looks after their assets. I used to absolutely hate having to go and visit him – now I am actually looking forward to seeing him. He will probably even call me by my first name, too!' They all laughed at the thought.

'We have to go over to Harrogate tomorrow, to attend to business,' said Tim. 'We have decided to keep the pub for the present at least. The solicitor has lined up some people for us to interview, with a view to installing new management – a husband and wife team to run it. I think it's an ideal place for the right couple. My solicitor and the brewery will keep a weather eye on things once we have settled the situation. I think it should work out fairly well.'

'That's a marvellous idea. I think it would be a pity if you sold it, Tim. You obviously put a lot of effort and time into it, and I have a sneaky feeling that you like the place rather too well to sell it if you don't have to,' Veronica said, nodding in approval.

'That is exactly what I told Tim myself, Veronica. Great minds think alike, as always!' Elizabeth said, grinning at her friend. 'California may prove to be great, but I think it is better to play safe, at least for a year, if not two. I am very excited about going there to live, but I'm not too sure about the TV station. Tim is, after all, heterosexual, and I am not entirely convinced that he will get the support of the management team at the station he will need at first. Tim does not fully agree with my point of view, but I just don't know.'

'Just because the management are – as far as we are aware – gay, does not necessarily mean that they will automatically resent me because I am not. I don't buy that. They have a station to run, and their livelihood depends on the success of the venture, so it won't pay them to create an atmosphere just because I am not gay. Business is business, and I am positive that they understand that the same as any other businessmen. Wait and see,' Tim said philosophically.

'I hope you are right, darling. It's just that I have never actually worked with a gay man before, and I honestly don't know what to expect, I suppose,' said Elizabeth, looking slightly embarrassed.

Tim laughed and said: 'They are just the same as you and me, silly. Their sexual preferences do not come into the equation when it comes to business, I am sure. My uncle George was an exceptionally nice man. You would have loved him.

'I know I am probably being silly. I just cannot help it. I am sure I'll be fine once we are in California and settle down,' Elizabeth said, trying to sound reassuring.

'How did you like the lawyer chap who took us out to Las Vegas?' Tim asked.

'He was a really nice bloke. You would like him, Veronica. So helpful too. Was he your Uncle George's lawyer for a long time?'

'I don't really know how long he was George's lawyer – I do know, though, that he was George's lover for the past five years.'

'Really?'

'I assure you he was. Now do you think that because the guys on the management team are gay that it automatically means disaster for me?'

'No – it's just that he was very straight-acting. I didn't guess. I feel rather foolish, now. California … Here we come!'

'That's my girl! We are going to love it, and I guarantee you that you'll love the weather. They don't call it the Sunshine State for nothing, you know,' Tim smiled and gave his wife a peck on her cheek. 'Veronica, you must keep your promise and come over and visit us in the off-season. Elizabeth should be feeling at home by then in San Francisco, and you'll both have a wonderful time. It is a very exciting city. I have been there a few times, and I loved it. So, whether business has been good, bad or simply mediocre, you are coming. Agreed?'

'Agreed – l have promised you I'll come over and l will. I am looking forward to it already. I don't know how you two manage to keep so calm about it all. It must be very exciting for you, and the speed at which it happened leaves the mind boggling. Has it all actually sunk in yet?'

'Now there is a question! You know I don't think the enormity of it has really sunk in yet. We are still in a sort of unreal dreamlike state, I think. Don't you agree, darling?' Elizabeth nodded in agreement. 'I put it down to jet lag, but I am not so sure now. I don't think it will sink in until we are actually in San Francisco. You will probably hear the scream over here when we do realise what has transpired!' Tim laughed.

'Well, when it does hit you, please remember the time difference, and don't scream too loudly. I wouldn't want you to waken my neighbours,' Veronica replied in her quiet droll fashion.

'Did Phillip say when he will be back? I would like to see him before we leave for the States.'

'No, Tim. He only said that he would be back in a few days. He did not put a specific time on it, I am afraid. I do know that he has to go to Scotland soon to film a programme but he did not say exactly when. Sorry if that's not of much help.'

'Not your fault. He has always been a rather vague chap, ever since he was a nipper. He'll probably turn up – that is, if he can tear himself away from your delectable sister.'

'Don't be such an insensitive brute, Tim!' Elizabeth scolded. 'Surely you can see that Veronica likes Phillip a lot and your remark was very hurtful. I suggest an apology is in order.'

'Oh! I am sorry, Veronica. I never knew that you were keen on old Phillip. I certainly did not mean to cause you any offence. I am an oaf. Please forgive me,' he said, looking very sheepish indeed.

'I never said that I was keen on Phillip! Where did you get such an idea, Elizabeth?'

'My dear Veronica, how long have we known each other? I knew from the first day we met Phillip that you were in love with him. You cannot hide it from me. I am sorry if I embarrassed you just now, but honestly, a blind man could see you are in love. I am surprised that Tim never caught on. Doesn't Phillip have any inkling how you feel about him? Hasn't he said anything to you?'

Veronica's face turned deep red with embarrassment.

'Am I so obvious? I thought that Cindy was the only one who had guessed. No is the answer to your question. And don't you dare say anything to Phillip when you do see him, or I'll never forgive you. And that goes for you as well, Tim. Promise?'

'You have our solemn promise, Veronica. If Phillip is too blind to see for himself, then that is his lookout. I honestly did not mean to embarrass you earlier. I am sorry.'

'That's all right, Tim. Think nothing of it. I just feel rather foolish thinking that I hid my true feelings so well and the only one l fooled was apparently myself,' Veronica said with a big sigh.

'I wouldn't say that. You fooled me completely. Perhaps you have fooled Phillip as well. Did you think on that?'

'What do you mean?'

'Well, you fooled me. I never gave it a thought that you loved Phillip. I never picked up on any signal. Perhaps Phillip hasn't either. He gives the appearance of the man about town, but I know him extremely well. He is actually quite a shy person when it comes down to serious matters on a personal level. Don't write your chances off just yet. That is my advice,' Tim said, giving her an encouraging smile.

'That is very nice of you, Tim. But I know when the opposition is too good. Melanie is quite a girl and she made it quite plain that she and Phillip have a good thing going. Thank you anyway – I do appreciate it. I'll just put the kettle on for some more coffee. Excuse me, please,' she said, and made her way to the kitchen, tears streaming down her face. She was angry with herself at losing control, and heartbroken at the same time. Love could be so cruel.

Elizabeth and Tim departed the following morning, promising to return in two days' time. The shop suddenly felt very empty. With both Elizabeth and Cindy gone, she felt loneliness for the first time in her life. She had of course been alone many times in her life, but this was the first time that she had actually experienced the sensation of feeling lonely. She busied herself dusting the stock, but the feeling refused to go away, and she heaved a big involuntary sigh. What a life, she thought, feeling rather sorry for herself.

'How much is this statue, ma'am?'

She looked up in surprise. She had been so absorbed in her own dismal thoughts, she had not heard the man enter the shop. 'I am sorry, sir. I didn't see you come in. Now, how can I be of service?'

She knew at that instant that she would never again allow her emotions to overpower her so, and she would certainly desist from indulging in self-pity, no matter what.

The day dragged for Veronica. The rain poured incessantly for hours on end with only an occasional customer to break the monotony. She was quite startled when Mr Stuart, the bank manager, came in. She had completely forgotten about him. His visit turned out to be very pleasant. Now that Veronica was on 'preferred customer' status with the bank, he proved to be almost human after all. He even lived up to her prediction, and insisted that she call him by his first name, David, and naturally he called her by hers. True to form, she reflected ironically, when he had departed.

That evening she decided to have an early night, and after her meal, she had a nice hot soak in a delicious bubble bath, and went to bed with a good romance story.

She fell sound asleep before she finished the first page, exhaustion catching up with her after the last hectic few days of excitement, and lack of sleep. The sun was shining bravely through the thin cloud cover as she opened up for business the next morning. It was a heartening sight after the dismal weather the district had been subjected to that spring, and she was feeling rather happier than she had of late. She looked up at the azure sky, with the promise of tempting tourists out of their hotels and into the shops at least.

A good night's sleep had worked wonders for her, and she put on the kettle with a song on her lips as she spooned the instant coffee into her cup, softly singing to herself. What a fantastic few days, she thought. No one would believe it if a writer used what had transpired as a plot for a novel. Truth really was stranger than fiction, she reflected.

The water was just coming to the boil when the shop door opened and the first customer of the day entered. A steady stream continued throughout the morning, and it took Veronica all her time to cope. What she would have given to hear the sweet sound of Cindy's voice, but she knew that she would just have to soldier on.

It was gone midday before she at last managed to have the promised cup of coffee, and boy, did she need it. She had just taken a bite of a salmon sandwich she had brought from the house that morning, when the door opened and a whole coach load of Japanese tourists inundated the premises. Ah well, so much for lunch, she muttered, and smiling broadly, approached the puzzled faces of the Orientals as they studied the prices of their potential souvenirs, tried gallantly to understand Veronica and struggled to convert the Sterling price into the more familiar Yen.

A lull around three o'clock in the afternoon at last provided the respite to enable her to finish her sandwiches, and enjoy a much needed pot of coffee. She had been absolutely dying for a cup.

She had just finished washing her plate and cup, when the shop door opened and a large heavy-set man entered and walked straight to the counter and demanded to know if she was Veronica Shillingworth. When Veronica replied, the man banged his fist on the countertop, demanding that she produce his daughter.

'Please calm down, sir. Yelling won't achieve anything. I have not the faintest idea of what you are talking about. Now, please be rational and explain calmly exactly what it is you want,' Veronica asked in a kindly tone, knowing full well what he wanted. She could not mistake the thick Australian accent, nor the uncanny resemblance.

Before her stood one extremely irate Mr Tom Crawford.

'Calm down? Calm down you say? Have you any notion who you are talking to? I demand that you tell me where my daughter is this instant, young lady!'

Once more he slammed his large fist on the counter.

'Sir, I request you leave my premises at once. When you have learned to keep a civil tongue in your head, you may return. Until then you are not welcome here. Now please remove yourself,' Veronica said quietly, although she was shaking in her shoes.

'How dare you speak to me like that! I demand an apology right now, and you will tell me exactly where Cindy is with the toe rag she has marrie …' His voice tailed off, he clutched his chest, his complexion turning red, and then slowly turning blue as he fell to his knees, mouthing something, but only silence came forth. Veronica dashed to him, as he fell to the floor.

There was no doubt in her mind – Cindy's father was suffering a heart attack!

Chapter Eight

Veronica cradled Mr Crawford's head in her lap. He looked at her from desperate eyes, and she heard him whisper something. She put her ear close to his mouth and she heard him whisper very faintly. 'Pocket … spray … pocket …' She followed his hand, and reached into the breast-pocket of his jacket, and removed a small white container. She looked carefully at the label, and followed the instructions. Removing the cap, she found a tiny spray mechanism, similar to a perfume spray. She opened his mouth, and sprayed two short bursts from the container under his tongue, as the instructions said to do. A strong aroma filled the air. A "hospital" smell was the only description she could think of to describe it later. Mr Crawford slowly began to breathe easier. He reached for the spray himself, and inhaled another burst of medication. A few moments later, he sat upright, and thanked Veronica for her prompt action.

'Please don't thank me. If you had not managed to whisper to me, l wouldn't have had a clue what to do and that, I am ashamed to say, is the truth. I am just grateful that you were able to tell me what to do. Are you sure you are going to be alright?'

'Yes. I'll be fine now, thank you. I am very sorry for my outburst. It was extremely rude of me, and quite inexcusable. Please forgive me.'

'You are forgiven. I know you must have had quite a shock to learn of your daughter's marriage. Can I offer you a cup of tea or coffee? Do you know what happened to you? Silly question! Obviously you know.' Veronica felt her face redden. Asking the obvious made her feel foolish, also she was not entirely sure that she should not have phoned for an ambulance, but Mr Crawford was adamant that he was quite recovered.

'That was an angina attack, I am afraid. The doctor told me not to get over-excited. That girl will be the death of me yet! Yes, I would like a cuppa, thank you. I really am sorry for my outburst, Miss Shillingworth. I can only apologise.'

'Please call me Veronica – and our little misunderstanding has been forgotten already. Are you quite sure that you don't need a doctor, Mr Crawford?'

'I am positive. Now, if I am to call you Veronica, then it is only fair that you call me Tom. Deal?'

'Deal. Please come through to the back shop. I'll put the kettle on. The tea will only take a moment. Now. I honestly don't know where Cindy is. I only know that she and Greg went to see his parents yesterday. In all the excitement I forgot to ask where they live. My business partner got married a few days ago as well, and she and her husband are going off to live in California. With everything happening at the same time, I forgot to ask Greg to leave his parents' address and phone number. That is the truth.'

'I believe you, Veronica,' Tom said as she handed him a cup of tea. 'She phoned me from his parents' home, and unfortunately I rather blew my top – gut reaction, I guess. Well, Cindy has a temper like mine, I'm sorry to say, and she hung the phone up on me before I had the opportunity to get the phone number myself. Fortunately, she had given me your address before I lost my cool. I flew to England immediately. I guess I am too late to have the wedding annulled?'

'I don't know the law, Tom, but I do know that Cindy and Greg would have something to say on the matter. They really are in love with each other. Greg is a very nice boy. Sorry, I had better say "man" or your daughter will have something to say about that too.' She smiled, and Tom Crawford let a hint of a smile cross his face for a moment too.

'I have tried to raise her to the best of my ability, but I never know what she is going to do next. I just couldn't believe my ears when she said that she was married/ The first thing that crossed my mind was that she had been nobbled by some blooming gold digger. What is this Greg really like? No kidding!'

'He is a very nice person, Tom – honestly. And I think you can set your mind at rest about him being a gold digger. He has just signed as a professional cricketer, and I imagine he will earn a fair living. I know he comes from a fairly well-to-do family. His cousin has told me a little about them, and they are not short of a bob or two. You know his cousin, come to think of it – Phillip Marden. You met him when he was in Perth reporting the Americas Cup.'

'Marden! No wonder the name seemed familiar. I knew it rang a bell, but I just couldn't place it. What does Phillip think of his cousin running off with my daughter?'

'He got as big a surprise as you, I think. We all did. When Cindy told me that she had eloped to Gretna Green, I thought she was pulling my leg. You could have knocked me over with a feather when I realised that she was serious. After a lot of arm-twisting, we persuaded them to go and tell Greg's parents, and they promised to phone you too. They were understandably nervous. Facing the consequences of one's actions is sometimes rather frightening. What seemed like a good idea can suddenly take on the dimensions of a Shakespeare tragedy. I felt really sorry for them but I was very relieved when they agreed to inform everyone, and get it over and done with. Once you accept the situation, I am sure that you will like Greg.' She suddenly realised that she had said far more than she had intended to.

'Cindy is a lucky girl to have a friend like you. You are a very wise person for one so young. And a very loyal friend too. You know, thanks to you, I am almost looking forward to meeting Greg. I guess if Cindy thinks he is so great, he can't be all bad,' Tom said, sipping the tea Veronica had made.

'I am still not entirely convinced that I should not have phoned for a doctor. Are you sure that you will be all right?'

'Honestly. I will be fine. You gave me the spray in time to prevent any real damage and I am grateful to you. l have never told Cindy about the angina, and I would appreciate it if you would keep this little incident just between us. Angina runs in the family, and I don't want to worry Cindy unnecessarily. Do you understand?'

'I understand your concern, Tom, but I don't know if I entirely agree. Cindy is a big girl now, and I think she would cope with your condition better than you think – but it is up to you, of course.'

'Well, perhaps you are right. I'll wait to see how things develop regarding her marital status etcetera. Then we'll see. What does Greg look like?' he asked, changing the subject.

'He is Phillip's double, only younger. You would take them for brothers rather than cousins, actually. The same broad shoulders and blond hair, and a good sense of humour too. He is also a fantastic cook, I discovered. He cooked a couple of meals when they stayed here for a few days, and they were absolutely first class. His cooking is a good as any top chef's.'

'Well, a good job one of them can cook, otherwise they would starve to death. Cindy can't even burn toast,' Tom said with a laugh. 'I spent a fortune sending her to fancy girls' schools, and she never even mastered how to cook the simplest dish. I guess that she is just one of those females that were never intended to be behind a kitchen sink. I wonder if her new husband has realised that yet? Should be fun when he does!' He laughed again.

'It is good to hear you laughing. I can see where Cindy gets her sense of humour from. Please try and meet Greg with an open mind. I know it is none of my business, but he is such a nice boy, and Cindy does love him so. I expect them back here within two days. Greg has to report to his cricket club soon, and they told me they would return at least a day before he has to report in. I probably shouldn't tell you this, but I have offered Cindy a job, and to stay at my house. You'll probably just get mad at me again,' Veronica said, crossing her fingers.

'No, I won't get mad again. One angina attack in a day is quite enough, thank you. Now that I know you, I am quite pleased that she will be staying with someone I have met and liked, I may say. Is the hotel any good? I noticed it on my way in. I don't really fancy driving any distance now, and it is handy to here. Could you be a pet and phone for me and see if they have a vacancy?'

'Certainly. I don't really know them, so I don't know how busy they are, but we'll soon find out,' Veronica said gaily as she picked up the receiver and dialled.

'I am sorry, Tom. They are fully booked, I am afraid. Listen – I know this is rather unorthodox, but I have plenty of room in my house, and you are welcome to stay.'

'I appreciate your offer, Veronica, but unfortunately I have a chauffeur with me. The car is a hired limo and the chauffeur comes with it. I have to supply him with a bed and meals. Normally not a problem. We'll just have to head for the nearest city and get something there.' He smiled kindly.

'Your chauffeur is most welcome to stay, Tom. I have plenty of room, honestly,' she replied, relieved that there would be someone else in the house too. In a small village, gossip could start with the slightest hint of scandal, and a man staying with her on her own was grist for the mill indeed! Two men ... now that could he interpreted in many ways, and was less likely to start the gossip mongers' tongues wagging.

'Are you quite sure?'

Veronica nodded in reply.

'I'll just tell the chauffeur to go for a coffee or a pint if he prefers. Where can he park the car?'

'Tell him to pull over to the house, and park beside my Mini. I'll phone the hotel again, and see if I can reserve a table for dinner.

Easier said than done, sometimes.' She immediately phoned the hotel, and to her relief, managed to reserve a table for eight o'clock. The meal was better than Veronica had anticipated. To be quite truthful, she confided in Tom, she had not really expected a very high standard. She explained the problems they had experienced trying to order simple takeaway meals, and the blunt refusal to serve them after eight o'clock. This was the first time she had actually eaten in the hotel, even though she had lived in the village all her life. Locals preferred the excitement of going to York or Harrogate, she explained.

'The grass is always greener on the other side, eh?' Tom said, smiling at his young companion. The chauffeur had preferred to have a bar meal, hence they were dining alone.

'I guess so, Tom. I think people are the same the world over. Talking about the world, Phillip seemed to really enjoy your home town. He said that Perth is a beautiful city. I have to admit, he made it sound wonderful. Cindy is very proud of it too. Being English, I find it strange when I hear someone praise their home town. We, as a race, seem to take delight in decrying all that is familiar – everything and everywhere else always sounds so much better. Perhaps that is why the British explored the world so extensively in the past. – never happy with what they had! We are still the same, I am afraid.'

'Young lady, you are an expert at keeping the subject away from the pertinent issue. Have you ever considered working in the diplomatic field? You are a natural!'

'Don't you think that you have had enough excitement for one day, Tom Crawford? I have deliberately steered away from Cindy and Greg. I certainly don't want to see you suffer another attack, thank you very kindly. Have you been to England before?'

'Yes, I have been here on many occasions – business of course. I have travelled the country fairly extensively, from the south of England to the north of Scotland. I even admit to liking your country, even if it does have the major drawback of being populated by Pommies!' He laughed.

'What a cheek! I heard that you positively quake in your collective shoes when England go into bat for the Ashes! Pommies indeed! At least we do not walk around upside down all day. Must have an effect on the brain, one would think,' she said, feeling rather pleased with herself.

She had had to work hard to think that one up – humour did not come naturally to her as it did to Cindy.

'Ah! Walking upside down all day long is very good for the brain cells, I'll have you know. Keeps the blood flowing to the head, therefore it keeps the brain better supplied with the food of life, and so naturally we Aussies have a far greater intelligence quota than you lot. Stands to reason, doesn't it?' he replied with a grin as wide as the Tasmanian Sea.

'I know when I am beaten,' she said. 'You win hands down, I would say. By the way, how was your flight over? Does flying not aggravate your angina?'

'The flight was fine, thanks. My angina does not act up as long as I take my medication prior to leaving. I am pretty careful about that, believe it or not. The plane is top class, with every mod con. I love it.'

'Do you pilot it yourself? ' Veronica asked.

'Wish l could. Unfortunately I can't fly jets. Even if I could, I wouldn't be allowed, because of the ticker. Too bad really – I would love to fly it.'

Veronica offered Torn and the chauffeur a drink when they returned to the house, but they both declined. The chauffeur excused himself and retired for the night. Tom had a cup of tea and a chocolate biscuit, and then he too retired. Veronica had another cup of coffee, and decided to go to her own bed; she was rather worn out.

Tom was sleeping soundly when Veronica popped her head in to his bedroom to check on him when she did not receive any response to her tapping on the door. The chauffeur was up and about. He had already showered and had gone out for a walk to buy a morning paper. He ate a hearty breakfast when he returned, and then asked Veronica to tell Mr Crawford that he was taking the car into Harrogate as he had instructed him to, and he would be back in about four hours. He bade her good morning and departed immediately in the beautifully presented Daimler. All very mysterious, she thought as she went to the shop to start the day's business. The weather was slightly overcast at first, but the sun broke through by mid-morning. A few people drifted in occasionally, but no major sales were made. In fact, all Veronica sold for the entire morning was a single postcard! Not exactly setting the world on fire, she mused. Tom Crawford appeared just after midday, freshened and full of beans after his long rest. Veronica spotted him coming and put the kettle on. He was talking into a mobile phone as he strolled the short distance to the shop. He paused at the door, and finished his conversation before entering.

'G'day Veronica, nice to see the sun can come out occasionally in England. I had a marvellous sleep, and I thoroughly enjoyed the cereal you left for me. How are you this fine day?'

'I am very well, thank you Tom. I'm glad you had a good rest. The flight here must be quite exhausting, no matter the creature comforts your plane provides. Your chauffeur has gone to Harrogate, and should be back quite shortly. He left about three hours ago.'

'Good. How's about a cuppa? I could murder one.' He smiled.

'Fancy a chocolate biscuit, or a nice cream cake?'

'Yeah. We'll have a nice cream cake, you and I. Where is the bakery?'

'The baker is down the street on the left. Are you sure that you are allowed a cream cake by your doctor?' she asked suspiciously.

'Of course. Every now and then, I have to eat something sweet to keep my sugar level up. Gives me energy, and I do love a cream cake.'

Veronica had the tea infused in the pot before he returned with a bag full of cream cakes, and two hot Cornish pasties.

'Couldn't resist them – they look and smell delicious.' He winked mischievously, and started to eat a pasty as he sat down in the back shop.

'I am positive that a Cornish pasty is not the best thing in the world you should be eating for lunch, Tom Crawford. But I won't say anything if you don't,' she said, taking a large bite from the other one as she spoke. Cornish pasties were a weakness of hers. She loved them, and made a point of avoiding the baker's shop most days to prevent herself from buying one. She simply could not resist them.

'You mentioned Phillip Marden being Greg's cousin. Is that how Cindy met him? Through Phillip, I mean.'

'No. Well, indirectly, I suppose. Phillip had been staying at a hotel not too far from here, and Greg had come up to visit him – the hotel Cindy was working at. Phillip had already checked out before Greg arrived. He met Cindy, and the rest is history. Love at first sight. I have said too much already – Cindy can give you the details herself. You must admit, it is all very romantic! One reads about couples eloping to Gretna Green but it is the first time I have ever known someone who has actually done it. I find it quite thrilling, to be honest.'

'I can think of a lot of ways to describe their actions, but thrilling is not high on my list. Irresponsible? Definitely! Romantic? Well, even I have to admit getting hitched at the famous Gretna Green does sound romantic. See, I'm not the old fuddy-duddy you had me down for. Even an old fool like me can have a romantic side. I suppose, given time, I'll accept the situation. Who knows, in enough time I may even get to like Greg. but don't you dare tell Cindy I said so! I'll tell you a secret: her mum and I eloped ourselves. Cindy doesn't know that. I just want to satisfy myself that she has not hooked up with a gold digger, and then I'll mellow. From what you have told me about young Greg, I am quite sure he is on the up and up. In fact, I'll probably like him. Anyone who plays cricket can't be all bad.' Then he added, with a wicked grin: 'Even if he is a Pommie!'

'Did I hear you correctly, Tom Crawford? Did you just say that you eloped when you were young?' Veronica asked incredulously. She couldn't have heard him correctly, surely?

Tom hung his head. 'You heard correctly. I have to admit that Marjory and I eloped, and to tell the truth I would do it all over again. Her father did not like me one iota, and we loved each other desperately so we took the only option open to us – we eloped. We never told Cindy. I don't really know why. The subject just never arose, I guess.'

'Then why on earth are you so put out about your daughter emulating what you have done yourself, and that you would do over again? I simply don't understand your logic, I am afraid.'

'We had our reasons, as I have explained. Her father was set against our romance from the start. I won't bore you with his reasons, but we were justified in doing what we did. Cindy had no reason that I can see for eloping. I, and indeed Greg's parent's, were completely in the dark as to their romance, therefore a clash of personalities, religion, or any other pertinent excuse that I can come up with simply does not apply. Perhaps you have an insight as to why they did what they did?'

'To be honest, Cindy never really went into detail. But from the little they told me, I think they felt that they simply could not live without each other, and if Cindy went home on schedule to finish her studies, they would not see each other for the best part of a year. I do know they did not go into marriage lightly. They spent many hours pondering their problem before they reached the conclusion they did. They do love each other with all their hearts. They must, to do what they did, and face the inevitable outrage of their parents. I imagine Greg's parents were as shocked as you were. Your daughter and their son are adults, and as such have the right to make and live their lives as they see fit. Love is a very powerful master. Surely I don't have to tell you that?'

'Love may indeed be a powerful master, Veronica. I wonder if my daughter realises what a powerful advocate she has in you? You put forth a powerful argument on their behalf. I do realise the power of love – could be that I had forgotten just how powerful love can be. You have brought back distant memories. I remember all too well how Marjory and I felt, and I am being a hypocrite condemning my daughter for doing the same as we did, and for feeling the same emotions, I guess. You know, it's funny – the shoe is on the other foot now, and for the first time I fully appreciate the way old Simon, Marjory's dad, felt. I might have got along a bit better with him if I had known then what I know now. Funny old life at times.' He smiled ruefully, and poured another cup of tea.

'And Cindy and Greg? Are you still going to give them a hard time?' Veronica asked.

'I just might huff and puff a little – for the fun, you know. But you have convinced me and I will accept the inevitable. If he is Cindy's choice, then he must be a bit of all right. She is my daughter, and if I cannot trust her judgement, then I have done a poor job of raising her. Thank you, Veronica – you have saved a lot of unnecessary strife,' Tom said sincerely.

'You have nothing to thank me for. Everything I said is only common sense, after all. I have no doubt that you would have realised that in time. Better before you face them to have come to terms with the situation. I am glad for you, Tom. You seem a lot happier in yourself.'

'Thanks to you, young lady. When this is over with, I am taking you for a slap-up meal. Cindy can watch the shop, and I am telling her that, married or not!' he said, the man of authority rising to the surface once again.

'I'll be glad to accept. It would be nice to have a little break from the shop. Excuse me, I'll have to go out front. I just spotted a coach pull into the car park. Hopefully some tourists will come my way. It has been very quiet today. She went into the front shop wearing her best smile.

Half an hour later, the till was a lot healthier than it had been. Sales were brisk for a period, giving Veronica a much-needed boost.

'Thank goodness for coaches' she said to Tom when the last of the tourists had departed for pastures new. 'I'd starve without them.'

'Are things that bad? I thought you had a nice little business going here.'

'The weather has been quite extraordinary this year. It has rained almost incessantly since Easter. Not too conducive for business in the holiday trade in general, I am afraid. Sorry, I don't mean to complain, but the weather can get one down at times. However, it has picked up the last couple of days, so here's hoping.'

'If you are finding things so difficult, you can't possibly employ Cindy. Charity begins at home is the old saying, but it does not, and cannot, apply to business, Veronica.'

'I need Cindy, Tom. Elizabeth, my business partner, is going to California to live, and we have adequate funding to see us through this bad spell. In England one learns to provide for the weather and its vagaries. Business will pick up as the weather does. You must excuse my rather morose mood – I guess I am still trying to come to terms with her imminent departure. I'll cheer up again pretty soon, you'll see.' The phone rang at that moment, and she excused herself in order to answer it.

'Well, that was someone you know on the phone. Cindy and Greg will be here in about two hours or so. That was Phillip, actually. They are travelling with him. I never told him that you were here. I thought it best not to.'

'You did the right thing, Veronica. I wouldn't want to run the risk of scaring the newlyweds off at this juncture. I promise that I will be very civil to them, and I will do my best to like Greg. He will be nervous, I know. I remember all too well when we went to inform Marjory's parents of the good news of our wedding. Talk about butterflies in the tummy. Boy, you don't know the half of it!' He smiled a rueful smile as he thought back on the fateful day.

Veronica was busy in the shop with an American couple when the Cadillac drew up outside, but gave Phillip a wave as he came in. She wore a slightly puzzled look as she wrapped their purchase. Phillip was alone. She thanked the couple and turned to face him. 'Where on earth are your passengers?' she asked him.

'Cindy and Greg got out at the other end of the village to do a spot of shopping. I guess you are wondering where your sister is?'

'Well, yes. But I was also looking for Cindy and Greg. Tom Crawford is in the back shop waiting for them – he arrived two days ago. I do hope that they won't be too long. By the way, just exactly where is Melanie?'

'The sight of two Rolls Royce and a helicopter parked at the front of the mansion was all the persuasion it took to spoil our romance, I am afraid. With Arabic royalty thrown in to boot, I had as much chance as a snowball in the Sahara,' Phillip replied with a huge grin. 'I was never under any illusions. I always knew that your sister was using me to access to powerful men in higher places than I will ever aspire to.'

'Then why on earth did you let her use you like that? I don't understand.'

'Sorry, I really should have confided in you. You see, Melanie overheard a conversation between the Sultan and the chap who produced the film that she was acting in Ireland. She was in the restaurant having dinner at the table next to them. They were quite unaware of her presence. She heard them planning their next project – a film to be shot in Brazil. The Sultan is the major stockholder in the film company the producer works for. She soon realised that I was a friend of Naseem's, and she made a play for me immediately. I am not so green between the ears that I don't know when someone is trying to manipulate me.

'I still don't understand why you let her use you, Phillip.'

'Let me finish, and you will understand, I promise. As you know, Naseem and I go way back to childhood. He has always been a practical joker, and being Sultan has not changed that. He has put one or two things across on me, much to his delight. I saw an opportunity to repay him. Melanie was the ideal answer for me. You see she thought – and probably still thinks – that she has used me to gain the introduction to the life she craved, in order to progress her ambitions. She never knew for a second that in actual fact – I am ashamed to admit because she is your sister after all – that I encouraged her advances. I planned every move. I knew she would make a play for Naseem the moment the opportunity arose. I simply arranged the moment. The rest, or rather, your sister took care of the rest. I bailed out quickly, and left Naseem with the delectable Melanie all to himself.' He beamed from ear to ear. 'One thing I forgot to mention to Melanie – it must slipped my mind. Naseem already has four wives!' He burst into fits of laughter. 'Serves them both right!' he blurted, doubling up in hysterics.

'You are cruel, Phillip Marden. It sounds as though Melanie will get the reward she deserves,' Veronica said, trying in vain not to laugh herself.

'Don't worry on Melanie's account. If I know her, she'll emerge from this with a nice fat contract for the film in Brazil,' Phillip said.

'What's all the laughter about?' Tom asked as he came from the back shop. He had been in the toilet and was not aware that Phillip had come in.

'Tom! Good to see you,' Phillip said, greeting him with a firm handshake.

'Good to see you again, Phillip. Where is my daughter and her new husband? I thought they were travelling with you?'

'They should be along any minute, Tom. They went for some shopping – they didn't know you were here. They shouldn't be too long.' He had no idea as to what Tom Crawford's reaction would be when Cindy and Greg did make an appearance.

The shop door opened and they all looked up expectantly, but it was a customer.

'Why don't we go through the back and have a cup of coffee?' Phillip suggested. Tom agreed and led the way. Veronica was showing the client out when Cindy and Greg came to the shop at last.

'How did you get on with your parents?' Veronica enquired of Greg.

'A bit dodgy at first, but Cindy soon had them eating out of her hand. About ten minutes was all it took for her to win them over,' he said proudly.

The tall figure of a man appeared from the back shop, scowling menacingly. 'And how long do you think it will take you to win me over, young man?' Tom Crawford demanded of his new-found son-in-law.

Chapter Nine

'Dad! Where on earth did you come from? You never told me you were flying over,' Cindy blurted out. She was so surprised, that for the first time in her life, she was stuck for words!

'Don't just stand there, Cindy. Introduce me to your husband. I take it this young man who seems to be rather taken with you is the individual?' he said in a gruff voice.

'Sorry. Yes, this is Greg. Greg, meet my dad,' Cindy said in a faltering whisper.

'Welcome to the family!' Tom said, a huge grin on his face. 'Congratulations!' He shook Greg's hand firmly, and then turned to his daughter and gave her a great big bear hug. 'Congratulations!' he said, and kissed her tenderly, as only a loving father can.

Greg and Cindy looked at each other in amazement. This greeting was the last thing they had expected. Tom looked them both in the eye, and told them that they had Veronica to thank. She had made him see sense before they arrived, otherwise they would have faced a very irate father.

'I hope you realise what a good friend you have,' he said. 'She is one in a million. Now, let's all go to the hotel this evening and celebrate. I'll pop over there right now and book a table, and woe betide them if they refuse because it will be after eight o'clock this evening!' He gave Veronica a broad smile. 'You know, if I was twenty years younger, I'd elope to Gretna Green myself!'

'You would?' Cindy said in bewilderment. 'With whom?'

'Veronica, of course!' He chortled to himself as he exited the shop, leaving four astounded people behind him. He turned back and popped his head round the door before anyone had a chance to react to his statement. 'Fancy a pint, Phillip? Greg is paying!' He beamed from ear to ear, as the two younger men looked at each other in astonishment.

'Well, what are we waiting for? Come on, Greg! Let's see what you are made of. Dig deep and treat your poor old father-in-law to a well-deserved pint.' He ushered Greg and Phillip from the shop, and led them to the portals of the hotel.

'Wow! I don't know what you have been saying to my dad, Veronica, but whatever it was, it sure worked. Thank you – you have saved our collective bacon. When he appeared from the back shop I almost died! I had not an inkling that he was here. I thought when I saw him he was going to hit the roof. I still can't believe how docile he is. Have you slipped him a sedative in his tea by any chance?' Cindy asked, half in fun, half in earnest.

Veronica knew that she would have to be careful what she said to Cindy – she did not want to betray Tom's confidence. She looked at her friend for a moment, and then started to laugh. 'Don't look so puzzled, Cindy. Your dad has simply had time to calm down and think things out since he arrived. He was pretty miffed when he got here, I must admit, but he listened to me prattling on about how much in love you and Greg are, and slowly his anger subsided. That's basically all there is to it,' she said with a shrug of the shoulders.

'Come on. I know from what dad said that you played a major role in making him see sense. I don't suppose you'll tell me. But I am very grateful, Veronica, truly!' she said and gave her friend a great big hug.

'I did nothing to deserve all this praise, Cindy. But thank you anyway. Your dad is quite a character, isn't he? I was really embarrassed when he made that comment about marrying me before he left the shop. One never knows what he will say next! Your life must have been fun growing up with him, or does he save that side of himself for the benefit of strangers?'

'No, that's what he is like all the time. He is great fun, and a really terrific person to be around. I bet you he has given Phillip something to think about with his remark! Maybe he twigged on that you have a thing for Phillip and has decided to gee him up a little. I know my dad!' Cindy laughed with delight as she imagined all sorts of fun and games to come.

'Don't say a thing like that, Cindy. He knows nothing of my feelings and don't you dare tell him either. If Phillip has any feelings for me, he can tell me without having to be cajoled into it. He mixes with too many beautiful women in his life to ever seriously consider me – I have told you that already. I have no delusions as to my own beauty, or lack of it, more like. I have my dreams, though, and I have the right to some privacy when it comes to them. I know that is as close to Phillip I will ever be. So please don't say or do anything to embarrass me.'

'I promise. I didn't mean to upset you, Veronica. I do wish you weren't so down on yourself all the time. You are a beautiful girl, you know. We can't all look like Melanie, or even want to. Don't judge yourself by her standards. That goes for most of the women that Phillip will meet on his TV programme too. They are professional beauties, that is they use what assets they possess to further their careers. What they lack in natural beauty, they pay some plastic surgeon to create for them. Personally, I'll reserve that treat for when I get on a bit and they start to sag!' she said with a peal of laughter, holding her breasts high.

'Wouldn't want to spoil your impact, my little beauties then, would we?' she added in pure devilment, fun twinkling in her eyes.

'You are the limit, Cindy!' said Veronica, tears of laughter rolling down her cheeks, the strain of the last few days dissipating in a moment's mirth. 'Does poor Greg realise what he has taken on, or is he still so infatuated that he can't see it yet? Poor soul – the penny will drop with a thud one day!'

'The penny will drop, did you say? More like a ton of pennies when he realises what he has got himself into! The poor soul still thinks I am wonderful. He'll wake up with a bang someday, when he finally succeeds in seeing that I am a woman, and not a goddess. What a shock he'll get! Never mind, love is all, so they say, so he'll still have everything his little heart desires, won't he?'

Cindy beamed a wicked smile. 'It is high time you got to grips with landing Phillip. You are far too placid. Get with it, girl. Put on some make up and make him realise that you are here, and available.

'If he doesn't get his finger out, he'll have some serious competition from my dad. Old Tom is quite a ladies man when he gets into the swing. Now wouldn't that be a bit of fun? l wonder if the old man has twigged that you have a thing for Phillip, and is giving him a gentle nudge?'

'Cindy! Don't say a thing like that! How could your dad possibly know that I like Phillip? I hardly mentioned his name,' Veronica protested.

'It is not only the female of the species that has intuition, Veronica. My old man can be pretty canny at times. I wouldn't be in the least surprised to learn that he knows about your feelings for Phillip. If he does, mark my words, he'll make a play for you, just to wind Phillip up. He's like that. What great fun! Relax – let the boys be boys. and sit back and enjoy the fun. You can only win, one way or another. Believe me. Phillip will be green with envy before he knows what has hit him. You'll feel like you are a film star quite shortly. Melanie, cry your eyes out, girl – your sister is about to show you how it is really done.' Cindy was laughing all the while, pure delight shining in her face as she let her imagination take over.

'What a girl! You really are the limit – utterly incorrigible. Have you ever stopped to consider the possibility that Phillip may not actually be in love with me? I think he would have made his feelings known to me by now, if he felt that way about me. You are living in cloud cuckoo land, Cindy.'

'Don't be such a pessimist, Veronica Shillingworth! After all, didn't Tim tell us that Phillip is a naturally shy person, and sometimes needs a prod in the right direction? And Tim is his best friend, and should know what he is talking about. I still say that he will turn green with envy if my old man makes a move on you,' Cindy said defiantly.

'When does Greg have to report to his club?' Veronica asked, anxious to change the subject. Her love life – or rather the lack of it – being the main topic was becoming slightly embarrassing.

'Tomorrow he reports in, and then two days later, he will have to get the old nose to the grindstone. So you will be having my undivided attention from then. Exciting prospect, isn't it?'

'I will certainly be glad of the help. It can get pretty hairy when a coachload of tourists appear from nowhere, with no warning. I know that I must have lost sales during the last few days. I am sure things will improve no end when you are here full time, Cindy,' Veronica said, glad that the subject had shifted direction at last. 'The weather is picking up a bit, so we should see an improvement in traffic flow, that is the amount of people who actually come through the shop, and hopefully a corresponding increase in sales.'

'No sweat, with me here to cajole the poor unsuspecting souls into putting their money where their mouths are. We are made! Come to think of it. I meant to ask you – has my old man bought anything from you?'

'Don't be silly. He has had far too much on his mind to think about presents to take home with him. I am sure he will buy something to remember here, when the time comes.'

'I'll make sure he does. By the way, when are Tim and Elizabeth coming back? I would like to see them again before they swan off to California. She must be a little apprehensive at the prospect of living out there – quite a difference from staying in rural England.

Are you planning on going out to see them during the off-season? If you are, Greg and I will come with you to Australia,' Cindy stated nonchalantly.

'As a matter of fact, I was thinking of going. Have you and Greg spoken about it then?'

'Get a grip, Veronica. He'll find out soon enough. Wouldn't want to spoil the boy's concentration before the season starts, now, would we?'

A coach drew up, and soon they were far too busy serving the requirements of three American men who were travelling together, reliving their war, they said. They were really knowledgeable about paintings, especially water colours. After a lot of discussion. they purchased no fewer than eight paintings between them. They paid in cash, and even insisted on tipping both the girls quite heftily, to thank them for their patience and help. Veronica was quite flabbergasted. Cindy just winked and told her when they had departed that she was on the job now, and sales of that sort of magnitude would be rather old hat by the end of the season.

'One thing is for certain. I'll never be able to say that you are short on confidence, Cindy. That was by far the largest sale I have had since the shop opened for business. I doubt very much if we can ever equal it again.'

'Of course we will equal, and surpass it, Veronica. Have a little faith. You carry a very nice selection, so why shouldn't you get – and expect – sales like that. Look on that as a target to set, and not as some freaky happening. As I said, you carry a beautiful selection for people to choose from, and not just a load of old rubbish. You should be proud of your buying skills and equally proud of your little shop.'

'Thank you, Cindy – it is very nice of you to say so. I guess that I tend to forget the careful work that went into stocking this place. Elizabeth and I spent many hours at trade fairs, and going around suppliers and artists, choosing the initial inventory. I am also still a little reticent when it comes to face-to-face contact with people. But I think l am getting there, albeit ever so slowly. You are lucky – you have a natural talent, and act perfectly naturally, whereas I simply act,' Veronica replied honestly.

Tom was as good as his word, succeeding where others had failed so miserably before him, in reserving a table at the hotel that evening. When Veronica asked him how he had achieved this feat, he simply held his forefinger to his nostril and winked.

'Natural ability,' he whispered. 'I like him!' he added under his breath, nodding in Greg's direction.

Veronica opened on time the following morning, her head thumping with a slight hangover. The champagne had flowed freely the previous evening. Tom Crawford had spared no expense, and the belated wedding celebration had gone on most of the night. Veronica had had to struggle to get out of bed in order to open on time.

Getting to be a habit, she mused, as she put the kettle on.

A car parked outside the shop, and two ladies entered.

Veronica could have seen them far enough at that moment, but she smiled bravely and spent twenty fruitless minutes trying to please them. Phillip came in just as they were leaving, and Veronica asked him if he could make coffee. He smiled broadly, and said he would be delighted to.

She marvelled at his constitution; he had been in pretty poor shape only a few hours previously, having celebrated rather too well with Tom. They had held a competition to see who could drink a bottle of champagne the quickest.

Phillip had lost, much to his chagrin. He simply could not consume so much at one time. He had duly paid Tom his one pound winnings, and then he passed out. Greg and his new father-in-law had carried the unfortunate Phillip over to Veronica's house and deposited him unceremoniously on the couch, and then returned to the party.

Tom had been rather impressed with his son-in-law. The more he saw of him, the more he liked him, he had confided to Veronica.

Cindy had overheard him, and was smiling from ear to ear, pleased that her father had accepted, and liked Greg. She too had taken Veronica into her trust, and confessed to overhearing the conversation she had had with Tom.

'I guess I can start to relax now. I was worried that dad might have found Greg too far out for his liking, but I know now that everything is going to be great. I can enjoy my party now. Have another glass of champers, Veronica – don't be so staid!' Cindy had said, pouring as she spoke.

Veronica came back to reality as she took the cup of welcome coffee gratefully from Phillip. She was paying for her own stupidity now.

'Will I never learn?' she asked as she sipped.

'Pardon?'

'Sorry, Phillip. I was just feeling sorry for myself. I drank a little too much last night for my own good. I was scolding myself out loud, I am afraid. I never seem to learn from past mistakes. Champagne is a weakness of mine, and I can't resist the temptation to indulge in one more glass. I am an idiot.'

'You are an idiot? I think I take the prize on that score! If I remember correctly, I bet Tom I could drink a bottle of the stuff quicker than he could. I don't seem to recall who won the bet, though,' he confessed.

'I am not surprised you don't remember, Phillip Marden! A man of your age being so silly. By the way, you lost,' she said with a smirk. 'You did have the presence of mind to pay your bet though, before passing out.'

'I must arrange transport. I have to get to my cottage today to get organised for the Orkney trip. I cannot possibly drive there myself – the drink won't have worn off yet, and I won't take a chance. Is there a taxi firm in the village, Veronica?'

'Yes, there is a part-time taxi service, but I really don't know if they would be prepared to hire a car and driver for the day. I'll phone and ask for you.' she said, taking out the Yellow Pages to look up the number. The door opened as she was speaking, and Tom came in.

'Good morning, you two. How is the head, Phillip? Hurt a little?' he asked, grinning from ear to ear.

'You are wicked, Tom. You know very well that it is your doing that poor Phillip is in the state he is in. You should be apologising, instead of gloating.'

'He is a grown man, and if he can't hold his liquor, he shouldn't make foolish bets,' came the retort, an even wider grin now on Tom's face.

'Perhaps so. But poor Phillip cannot drive home to organise himself for his next trip for his TV show. I am just trying to arrange a taxi for him.' She continued thumbing through the pages as she spoke.

'Don't bother with a taxi. I have a limo and driver sitting doing nothing. He'll take you, and bring you back Phillip. You are coming back today, I hope?'

'Yes, I'm coming back, Tom. I'll have to collect my car when I am fit to drive later on today. I appreciate your offer of the use of your car and driver. You have just saved my skin. Thank you.'

'No sweat – after all, it is seemingly my fault you cannot hold a little champagne so it is the least I can do!' he replied, winking teasingly for Veronica's benefit. 'A man could die of thirst around here waiting to be asked,' he added, thoroughly enjoying kidding the life out of Veronica.

'One thing still puzzles me, Tom. Just how did you persuade the hotel to serve us a meal so late in the evening?' Veronica asked.

'Well … seems that some company from California made them an offer they couldn't resist yesterday, and they sold out to them.

Some guy from an inn around this area was sent to run the hotel for a few days until the new owners arrive to install a management team. The opening times were changed immediately on take-over. I couldn't resist taking you all for a ride, saying it was my charm. It was the charm of the dollar bill that spoke volumes. I wonder who the new owners are?'

'I think I perhaps know the answer to that,' said Veronica. 'In fact, I am sure I do. Tim had such a hard time with the hotel owner, I would not be surprised to learn that he is the mystery buyer. He does own a hotel chain in the States now, and has the financial muscle to swing a deal like that overnight. What do you think, Phillip?'

'Highly possible that you have hit the nail on the head, Veronica. Tim has the kind of nature that would make him shift heaven and earth to prove a point, and if the hotel owner annoyed him so much, he would do something like buy him out. I think you're right.' He nodded his head in agreement.

'Good morning, all,' Cindy said as she breezed in, smiling pleasantly. Now, if you are all going to stand around here, it is going to cost. We have a business to run. Now then dad, dig deep and buy a few little trinkets to take back to Oz with you. No time like the present to stock up!' she said bossily. 'We have a wonderful collection to please all tastes. Phillip – did I hear you say you were thinking about buying your parents a painting of this locality? Come on, boy. Don't think you are getting off Scot free – produce your wallet, shake out the cobwebs, and give the moths a fright!'

Phillip made a hasty getaway, breathing a sigh of relief as he got into the car. Tom laughed, and told his daughter to make a selection of gifts for him to take home, and he too beat a hasty retreat to the safety of the hotel bar.

'That cleared them out of the way,' Cindy commented as she poured coffee for herself and Veronica. 'You are far too soft with those men. You really must learn to tell them to clear out of the shop during business hours. They will walk all over you otherwise.'

'You are probably right, Cindy – in fact I know that you are right of course, but I don't have the heart to tell them. Thank you,' Veronica said, smiling to herself at her friend's audacity, and the instant response it had produced.

'How did Greg survive the evening's festivities?'

'Not too well. He put on a good show last night, but it has caught up with him. I'll let him rest. He has to report to his cricket club tomorrow, and he had better appear looking at least sober, if not fit,' she said with a giggle.

The morning passed quickly, with a steady flow of customers coming through, much to Veronica's delight. Cindy was a boon indeed. Her nonstop chatter, friendly smile and helpful suggestions kept the till ringing very nicely. Whatever had she done without her? That question was foremost in Veronica's thoughts as she put the kettle on for lunch.

'Is Phillip returning this evening?' Cindy asked.

'Yes – he has to pick up his car. He should be fit to drive himself by then. Your dad very kindly offered him the use of his limo and driver for the day. I thought Phillip was going to kiss him when he offered.' Veronica laughed.

Tom insisted that Veronica took an hour off to have lunch at the hotel with him. Cindy looked after the shop, being even more insistent than her dad had been. Veronica relented, and luxuriated in the sheer pleasure of having a cooked meal for lunch for the first time in ages. Tom was marvellous company, keeping her in stitches most of the time as he reminisced about his early days in business, and the close calls he had financially as he took risks against his bankers' advice, with the threat of bankruptcy ever present, but he had triumphed in the end. He made it sound very easy and very comical, but Veronica realised that he must have had nerves of steel to do what he did. Quite a man!

Elizabeth and Tim were in the shop when they returned from lunch. Elizabeth explained that they were leaving for California in the morning, and had come to say their farewells. Everyone was very emotional, but as Tom quickly pointed out, California was only a few hours away by air, so what was everyone getting so excited about?

Elizabeth told Veronica that she and Tim were staying with her mum that night, but promised to come to Veronica's house around nine o'clock in order to say goodbye to Phillip. They then left the shop to go to her mother's and Tom excused himself saying he had a few things to attend to before evening.

'I wonder how Greg is up to? We haven't seen or heard from him, come to think of it. Did dad happen to mention Greg to you, by any chance?'

'No. His name never came up, I am afraid. Why don't you phone the house and make sure that he is all right, Cindy?'

'Tell you what – you hold on here for a moment and I'll pop over and see if he is there, and find out what he is doing,' Cindy replied, and was gone before Veronica could answer.

'He is not there, and there is no sign of my dad either. I wonder what they are scheming?'

'What makes you think that they are scheming something?'

'I know my father too well. They are up to something, and he is behind it,' Cindy replied.

'Wait a minute! You have forgotten something, you silly girl. Didn't you tell me yesterday that Greg had to report to his club the next day?'

'What a fool I am – of course he does! How could I forget that? I must be getting over the hill. But his bike is still here. Look, it is sitting across at the house. I do hope he has not forgotten as well.'

'I doubt that very much. Far too important a thing for him to forget, I should say,' Veronica replied. 'Here is your dad coming – perhaps he can shed some light on the mystery.'

'Dad, do you know where Greg is?' Cindy blurted out as soon as her father put his foot inside the door.

'Don't tell me that you don't know where your own husband is? I thought that you would keep better tabs on him. You surprise me, Cindy. He has probably just realised what he has done, and that he is actually married, and taken fright and beaten a hasty retreat!' Tom said with a smile.

'Very funny, I'm sure!' Cindy replied crossly. 'Do you know where he is? He has to report in to his club today. He must have forgotten! Please, dad. Have you seen him?'

'Stop worrying. He is safely at the ground by now. He took a lift in the car with Phillip. They are picking him up tonight. I thought that you knew. Honestly,' her father said, holding his arms in surrender.

'What a relief! I'll throttle him when he returns – he should have told me.'

'Blame me. I asked Greg to do a little errand for me. He probably forgot to tell you that he was going in with Phillip in all the rush. I should have thought. I am sorry, dear,' her dad said, bowing his head.

'Just what could he be doing for you that is so important that he would forget to tell me that he was leaving with Phillip? I can't buy that. You are making excuses for him.'

'No, Cindy, I am not making excuses for him. He is doing something very important, very important. You'll find out when the time is right, so don't go quizzing him tonight.'

'What? You are joking – surely you cannot possibly expect me to stay silent? Nothing can be that important!' she fumed.

'I made Greg swear to secrecy. Now, you wouldn't make a man break his word, would you?' Tom asked.

Cindy looked at her father for a long time. 'This had better be a beaut of a reason, or the two of you will land in Oz without the aid of an aeroplane,' she said. 'Secrecy indeed!' She huffed.

'That's the spirit! Thanks, dear, ' Tom said, kissing his daughter on the cheek. 'You are very quiet, Veronica.'

'I don't want to get involved in a family tiff, Tom. After all, it has nothing to do with me. But I do feel that at least one of you should have told Cindy. She has been worried sick wondering where on earth Greg had got to.'

'I know. I do apologise. But I honestly thought that Greg had told her, as I have already explained.

Can't stay and gossip, I am afraid. Pressures of work and all that, you know,' he said with a grin and promptly left the shop before either of the two girls could reply.

'That is just typical of my dad. I wonder what he is up to? Greg is obviously up to his ears in the conspiracy. That is why he never told me he was leaving with Phillip this morning. Too frightened he would let something slip,' Cindy surmised, correctly as it turned out.

'Men! They can be very exasperating at times. I suppose we'll find out when it suits them to tell us what they are up to. Phillip is probably up to his neck in it too,' Veronica said.

'He was very quiet when he left. They are probably planning on going to a football match and waiting until they have the tickets before saying, so they have a valid excuse to go.'

'You know, you could be right, Veronica. That is the sort of thing my dad would do. "Can't expect us to waste all that money, can you?" That is his patent excuse for everything he does that he doesn't want me to be part of.' She folded her arms in consternation.

'Look on the bright side – it should prove fun making the boys tell what they have been up to when they return. We can make them squirm,' Veronica said with more than a hint of devilment in her tone.

'Yeah – let's really make them squirm! That will teach them to play with our feelings. We will pretend that we are mad at them and not talking to them, and blame my dad. We'll make him squirm too. He deserves it!'

Tom stayed well out of the way for the rest of the day, much to his daughter's annoyance. She was really determined to make him confess what he and the boys were up to, but never got the opportunity. Veronica just smiled at Cindy's plight, and told her more than once that patience would pay in the end. Cindy merely huffed and puffed. She hated being in the dark about anything, and her father knew this, and no doubt he was taking great delight in teasing her. She just knew he was, and this annoyed her even more.

Phillip and Greg appeared at the shop shortly before five that evening. They breezed in as large as life, both delighted with their respective efforts of the day. Their good humour was soon put to rest as they were assailed by a very irate Cindy. Poor Greg stammered and stuttered as he tried to calm his wife, and avoid telling her what he had been doing for his father-in-law – not an easy task. Phillip did his best to calm her, and tried changing the subject by asking where Tom was.

'That is what we would all like to know!' Cindy retorted.

'Aren't you going to ask me how I got on today, dear? After all this was my first day,' Greg inquired of his rather irate wife.

'I am sorry darling, but I just know that my dad has had the two of you up to something, and it is killing me. I simply cannot help myself. How did you get on then? Bowl them for six?' Cindy replied.

Greg shook his head and laughed. 'I got on just fine, thank you. I admit that I did a little errand for your dad, Cindy, but it was no big deal. He'll tell you about it himself when he has at mind to, I am sure. Now why don't you tell me about your day?'

Cindy immediately swung her attentions to Phillip: 'What were you doing for my dad, Phillip?' Experience had taught her that a change of tack sometimes achieved results. This time she was to be disappointed.

'Nothing really. Only took about ten minutes or so.'

'Oh! I give up!' Cindy fumed, and went to the back of the shop to put the kettle on, accepting inevitable defeat.

Veronica laughed as Greg pulled a face behind Cindy's back. 'I guarantee you would be too chicken to repeat that when your wife comes back through here,' she said to him.

'Too right I would!' he said, laughing to himself.

'Now, if I were not a lady, I could threaten to tell her what you did unless you tell me what you have both been up to today,' she said with a smile on her lips.

'You are too nice a person to resort to blackmail, Veronica. I am surprised and shocked at you even contemplating such a thing,' Greg replied with mock hurt in his voice. 'Aren't you shocked, Phillip?'

'Very much so, Greg. I never knew the female of the species could be so vindictive,' he said, shaking his head in mock sadness. 'Tom would be extremely annoyed and dismayed, I have no doubt, if he knew what we were enduring just because you and I are gentlemen and did him a little favour, and are keeping our word to remain silent. What we have to suffer is nobody's business for the price of loyalty.'

'Give it a rest you two, or you'll never get another cup of coffee in this establishment again. And that is a promise, not an empty threat,' Veronica said, shaking her fists at them, and trying not to laugh.

Cindy was serving coffee when the door opened and her dad came in to the shop, grinning 'What are you looking so pleased with yourself for? I am still not speaking to you, you know,' his daughter said as he entered the premises. 'I suppose you smelled the coffee?'

'What a wonderful suggestion, oh daughter of mine. Cream and two sugars please,' Tom said, winking to Greg. 'I don't suppose you would be in the least bit interested in what your husband has been doing for his dear old father-in-law?'

'That is the last thing in this world that Cindy would want to know, Tom. Curiosity is not one of her vices, and she would never think on trespassing into yours or my private business. Being her father I am surprised that you don't know that,' Greg said with a straight face.

'Silly me! I should have realised that no daughter of mine could ever let curiosity get the better of her. I do apologise,' Tom replied.

'Will you guys knock off the comedy routine and please tell me just what you have been up to?' Cindy blurted, her face turning slightly purple.

'Not a lot really,' her father replied nonchalantly. 'Greg simply picked up a little item for me on his way home. I believe it is at the rear of Veronica's house.'

'What on earth is it then?'

'Why don't you pop over and take a gander? We will look after things here. Go on then. Shake a leg!' her father commanded.

A few moments later Cindy and Veronica arrived at the rear of the house, and there, in all its glory sat a child's scooter, with a tag which bore the inscription: "Now you are a married lady, I thought you would appreciate your very own transport. Love, dad".

Chapter Ten

Veronica fought the tears back as she thought about Elizabeth. They had said their goodbyes two days before, as Elizabeth and Tim had set off to begin their new life in California. Veronica hated saying farewell – she had been friends with Elizabeth since school days and would miss her terribly. Phillip was in Scotland, filming his new series of fishing programmes, and Cindy was in Durham with her dad watching Greg play cricket. Suddenly the shop seemed a very lonely place after all the excitement and activity of the past few days, and Veronica was feeling rather sorry for herself.

A coachload of Japanese tourists kept her occupied for a while, and then Elizabeth's mum came into the shop to boast about the absolutely wonderful husband her daughter had won for herself, and rub the point home that it was too bad that Veronica would have to settle for the life of a spinster. After all, she could hardly expect to land a husband at her age! Plain women just had to accept that the single life was probably the life that was intended for them, so why fight it? Veronica could have gladly strangled her by the time she left. Come to think of it, Elizabeth was a year older than her – what a cheek that woman has, she fumed inwardly.

A broad smile suddenly spread across Veronica's face as she thought about Cindy's expression when she found the child's scooter that Tom had bought her. She was absolutely stunned and quite a few seconds passed before she noticed the note taped to the handlebars.

She beamed from ear to ear when she read the message, and handed it to Veronica to read.

Veronica read the note, and smiled. 'Your dad certainly has a sense of humour, Cindy. "If you grow weary pushing this, you could try and find the vehicle which the keys (attached to the underside of the scooter) fit. Good luck!" Veronica smiled as she finished reading the note aloud.

"PS – I am glad you married Greg, even if he is a Limey! Dad."'

Cindy made her way to the other side of the building, where a beautiful new MG sports car was sitting. Fire-engine red, as all sports cars should be. Running to the car, Cindy tried the key in the door, and sure enough, it fitted.

'Wow! Good old dad!' she said as she opened the door and sat in the driver's seat. A note was taped to the steering wheel, which congratulated her and Greg on their wedding and said that this was a little token of love from a dad who doted on his daughter and a proper wedding gift of a new house would be coming their way, as soon as they decided where they were actually going to live.

Veronica thought how marvellous it must be to have a father who could afford to purchase a house for his offspring's wedding gift – Cindy was a very lucky young woman indeed.

Phillip had been away for three days now. Veronica was quietly surprised at how much she was missing him. She did love him dearly, but she had resigned herself to settling for his friendship, platonic though it might be. He was wonderful company, and she would rather have his friendship than run the risk of declaring her love for him, and possibly be rejected, therefore losing his friendship.

Too big a risk for her to even contemplate. She smiled as she thought of Phillip's private confession to her, prior to his departure, he was going to Scotland on a sea fishing trip, and that he suffered from chronic sea sickness.

Poor Phillip, he must be suffering so! He had not dared tell the others – they would have teased the life out of him.

'The price of fame and fortune,' he had mused, rather wishing that he was going to a burn in the highlands fishing for brown trout. Far easier on the tummy, and a lot safer too.'Don't be a scaredy cat, Phillip. I read that sea sickness is mainly in the mind, so think positive, and I am sure that you'll be fine,' Veronica had said comfortingly, rather glad that she did not have to go, as she suffered from the same affliction.Cindy was even more excited about Greg making his debut than he was himself. She was so nervous before they left that she had to take a tranquiliser, much to Veronica's surprise. She had never thought of the light-hearted Cindy, always ready with a quip, getting herself into a state like that. Greg, on the other hand, seemed as calm as could be – if he was feeling nervous, he certainly hid it well. Tom cracked jokes in his inimitable manner, trying his best to keep everyone cool and collected. He had them all laughing as they got into the car to make their way to Durham. Veronica envied them, but she had to look after the shop, and she honestly had no regrets about that.

Business had been doing very nicely over the recent weeks, pleasing her no end. All the hard work, disappointment almost verging on the downright depressing, was all forgotten. Life really was sweet. The only thing missing was Phillip! She sighed to herself – at least she had his friendship. Love really could be cruel as well as the most beautiful thing in the world.

She stared out of the window at the hotel opposite. Big changes were taking place over there even as she observed an American couple who had been in her own shop earlier that morning, entering the hotel doorway. Tim had indeed purchased the business from the proprietor, and had immediately brought in professional management to bring it up to the standard that one expects from a hotel.

Much to Veronica's surprise, he had invited her to sit on the board of directors of the hotel. He had set up a company separate from the hotel chain his uncle had bequeathed him in the States.

He explained that he preferred to keep his little bit of England in England. He also said that he would look on it as a great favour if she would accept the position as a director. That way he would feel more confident about his purchase with someone on the spot to keep a weather eye on things. Veronica was delighted to accept the offer, and indeed felt very privileged that Tim was confident enough in her to ask. She couldn't help but feel a little pride.

A manager had been installed, hired through a professional consultancy company. A team of experts were flying in from the States in the next few days, on loan from Tim's American hotel chain, to sort out any problems and plan a modernisation programme. Veronica was very excited at the prospect of the village having a top-class hotel at last. It was long overdue, she felt. A maroon-coloured Rolls Royce drew up at the door of the shop, drawing her attention. One could not help being attracted by a Rolls Royce! A dark handsome Arabic looking gentleman alighted, and entered the premises.

He smiled broadly. 'You must be Veronica,' he said, extending his hand. 'I am Naseem, Phillip's friend. I have heard so much about you, I feel that I know you already.' He flashed a dazzling white smile. 'Phillip was quite correct – you do not look like your sister. You are far more beautiful.'

Veronica blushed to her roots. She was not used to such compliments. 'I am so pleased to meet you, your Highness,' she said in an awestruck whisper.

'Call me Naseem – please. No formalities when amongst friends. I assume Phillip is in Scotland? Have you heard from him?'

'Yes, he is in Scotland, and no I have not heard from him.'

'That is so like Phillip. So engrossed in his work. He totally forgets to keep in touch with the woman he loves. I really must have a word in his ear. Love is the first priority in life – everything else is secondary. I am sure you would agree with that?' He flashed that devastating smile, his dark eyes twinkling with obvious delight at Veronica's embarrassment. 'I am sure you must have misunderstood Phillip, or perhaps I misunderstood you. Did you say that I am the woman he loves?'

'Oh! Don't tell me I have put my foot in it? Do you mean to tell me that the poor boy still has not had the courage to tell you that he loves you? I am so sorry, Veronica. I do apologise for speaking out of turn. I most certainly did not mean to cause you any embarrassment.'

Veronica just stood in stunned silence, Phillip does love me, she thought with delight, even though the news of his love came in a most unorthodox fashion.

'No need to apologise. I have loved Phillip since the first time I saw him, but never dared hold out any hope that he could possibly love me. He is a very shy person underneath, I know that, but I never dreamt that he loved me. You have made me very happy. Thank you, and I promise not to tell Phillip what you said. I would like to hear the magical words from him – without any prompting!'

'You are very gracious. Now down to business. I find I must return to my country in a few days, and I would like to purchase a few trinkets to take back. Phillip has told me of the wonderful stock you carry, and I thought l would come and see for myself. I would like some pottery, preferably made locally if possible.'

An hour and a half simply whizzed past, with a huge list of purchases piling ever higher on the counter. The 'few trinkets' now totalled over three thousand pounds, and he was still buying. 'My shopping list seems to grow with every trip I make to England. I am always promising myself that I will cut down the next time, but it never seems to work out that way. I love this silver tankard. Can you have an inscription done for me?'

'Of course.'

'I would like to have the Royal Coat of Arms inscribed. I would require a fairly large number, though.'

'How many?' Veronica asked, expecting her rather welcome and extravagant client to request two or three dozen.

'Six hundred to begin, if the court approves of the design – we use tankards to drink goats' milk on festive occasions,' he explained, 'then the total will probably exceed three thousand or so.'

Veronica's mouth gaped in astonishment. 'When you throw a party, it must be something else!' she gasped.

'The tankards will be used at official occasions and religious festivals only. They will contain goat's milk. That is the traditional drink of celebration in my country.'

'I see. But I think it only fair to point out that you would save a considerable amount if you ordered them straight from the manufacturer,' Veronica said.

'I appreciate your honesty, but I wish to give you the business. I am not concerned with money matters, I am only concerned with the fact that I like the tankards, and that you can supply the quantity required,' he said, smiling broadly and displaying a perfect row of brilliant white teeth.

'I assure you that I can arrange any quantity you desire, and within the time limits you set.'

'Excellent! Now let us dwell on more pleasant things. I would be honoured if you would be so kind as to dine with me this evening.' He waved his arm almost imperceptibly as he spoke and the chauffeur entered the shop. 'Please take care of my purchases and arrange payment, Ahmid.'

'Your Highness,' Ahmid replied, bowing deeply.

'I would be delighted to have dinner this evening, but I have already arranged to dine with Cindy and Greg, along with Cindy's father, to celebrate Greg's debut in first class cricket.' Veronica replied.

'Of course! How remiss of me. I insist that you all be my guests this evening. I must pay my respects to Greg. Congratulations are in order. I have reserved a suite in the local hotel. Please convey my regards to Greg and his family, and be so kind as to convey my invitation. I believe nine-thirty would be suitable to allow for the long hours your shop is open?'

'Nine-thirty is fine – thank you.' Veronica replied, still in a daze. He bowed slightly and took his leave. Ahmid requested the total of the purchases, and opened the briefcase he was carrying, and paid in cash – over four thousand pounds in total, not including the pewter tankards.

'His Highness shall inform you tomorrow of the date the first shipment will be required. Please relay the amount of money you require to pay for the first order, including shipping charges to me in the morning, Miss Shillingworth. His Highness insists that you receive payment in advance.'

He held up his hand as Veronica made to protest. 'His Highness insists.'

Veronica watched the door close as Ahmid took his leave. She was in a daze, and had to pinch herself to make sure that she had not been dreaming. Suddenly she realised just how much cash she had in the till, and nervously removed the crisp hundred-pound notes and placed them in her handbag for safety. She had never held so much cash in her hands before, and it made her a little edgy.

Veronica sat at the dressing table, looking at herself in the mirror. It was not a pretty sight! She had eventually climbed into bed at the unearthly hour of four-thirty in the morning, and her reflection showed all too well the ravages that the preceding night had inflicted upon her. Too little sleep and too much champagne had taken their toll. Never again, she vowed, as she ran a brush through her hair, causing her to wince as the pain shot through her head.

But what a night it had been! A great time was had by one and all. Naseem had spared no expense. After they had dined, he had ordered champagne for not only their party but for all the hotel guests as well. The village had never seen such magnanimous generosity, and the French Queen of Wines had flowed freely as one and all took advantage of his magnificent gesture. The festivities were still in full swing when she excused herself at four in the morning. Phillip would have enjoyed the occasion so much, she thought, as she prepared tea and toast for breakfast. What a pity he could not have been there. She heaved a sigh, biting into the toast with little enthusiasm. She sipped a little tea, trying to convince herself that a good breakfast was an essential start to the day, and she would feel the better of it, want it or not.

She was opening the shop door when Cindy appeared at her side, her usual bright and breezy self. 'How on earth can you look as though you have just had a good night's sleep, Cindy, when I know perfectly well that you have not even been to bed? I do envy you. I feel as though I have been dragged through a wringer backwards.'

'You simply lead too sheltered a life, sport. High time you loosened up a bit, my girl,' Cindy answered amiably 'I see I must have a word with Phillip when he returns,' she added with a touch of devilment.

'Don't you dare do such a thing!' Veronica blurted. 'I'll have you know that I have had my moments, too – I am not as naive as all that.' Her face turned a light shade of pink, making her lie obvious.

'I'll believe you, though I am quite sure that thousands wouldn't,' Cindy replied, tongue in cheek.

'You really are incorrigible. Cindy! Let's get the shop open and the show underway,' Veronica said, turning the key in the lock as she spoke and smiling broadly. She suddenly turned on her heels and spun to face Cindy. 'Greg! Where on earth is he? Shouldn't he be at the cricket ground?'

Cindy laughed as she looked at the frown on her friend's brow.

'Don't worry, Veronica. Greg popped out from the festivities before midnight, and went to the house to catch his beauty sleep. He must have been in bed snoring his head off when you eventually dragged yourself over. He dropped into the hotel for a bite of breakfast this morning before he set off. But it is really nice of you to remember. Wouldn't have made a great impression if he didn't show up on only his second day, now would it?'

'I'm relieved to hear that. I was worried for a moment. I must have had more than my fair share of champagne last night. I had no idea that he had left the party, nor any inkling that he was in the house when I managed to stumble over there. What would my dear old mum say to that, I wonder?'

They were still giggling as they put the kettle on for the first cup of coffee of the day.

Ahmid entered the shop just as they were settling down to savour the hot coffee that was steaming in their cups. 'Many pardons for interrupting, ladies,' he said in his heavy accent, 'but His Highness has instructed me to ask you if you would do the great honour of joining him for lunch today?' He flashed a brilliant white smile, and bowed deeply.

Veronica and Cindy glanced at each other and then Veronica replied that they were very honoured indeed, but could he please send their apologies to his Highness, as it was impossible to close the shop during lunch. Ahmid bowed once more, and said he would tell his Highness and relay their most profuse apologies. He exited the premises as silently as he had entered.

'Too bad. I think we just blew the fanciest lunch we never had,' Cindy sighed.

'I know you are right, but I honestly cannot close the shop – but you are most welcome to take up the offer, Cindy. Honestly.'

'No way, but thanks for the offer. We either both go, or both stay, and that's that. My dad will say that we are a couple of idiots when he finds out.'

'I really don't think so. He is a businessman and he fully understands that business is business, and must take precedence over pleasure.'

'Yeah, I know you're right. Oh Well. I suppose it's the old bread and water regime again. Farewell the good life. But man, it was something else while it lasted!' Cindy winked at her friend, smiling broadly.

The morning was – much to the girls' relief – fairly quiet, giving them time to recover somewhat from the "night before" syndrome. Veronica swore that she would never again imbibe to the extent that she had done the previous evening. She hated having a headache and not being in top form for the day's work, and scolded herself severely.

The village clock chimed twelve noon, and Cindy said that she could take a hint, and went through the back shop and put the kettle on.

'I am looking forward to a nice cup of coffee and a light lunch,' Veronica said. Just as she spoke, the front door opened, and three waiters from the hotel entered, carrying silver trays laden with food.

A smiling Naseem followed the entourage, waving his arms and stating that he could not possibly leave his favourite beautiful girls to starve. The waiters progressed to the back shop and spread a table fit for a queen – two queens in fact. Both girls gasped in unison.

'Naseem, I don't know what to say. This is simply splendid!' Veronica said, shaking her head with awe.

'The very least l can do for such dedicated business ladies. I admire you greatly for putting your business first. I now know beyond any question that I made the correct choice when I invited you to have my tankards made for me. They are very important to my court and my people, Veronica, and I am now filled with confidence that you shall fulfil the order to the letter.

My congratulations, my dear.' He smiled sweetly and then said: 'Let's stop talking so much, and use our mouths for what they were intended by Allah to do. Let us eat.'

The meal thankfully was enjoyed without interruption.

'I can't believe that we have actually had time to have such a wonderful lunch without a coachload of tourists barging in,' Cindy said, reaching for yet another chocolate éclair.

'I simply do not know where I put it,' Veronica said, 'especially after last night. Thank you once again, Naseem, the meal was wonderful and you are right, Cindy – I cannot remember when we last had a free half hour to enjoy our lunch.'

The front door opened as she spoke and an entire coach of Japanese tourists entered enthusiastically, all smiles and all wearing the obligatory camera around their neck. Cindy and Veronica glanced at each other, and could not help laughing. Fortunately, the potential customers took this as a sign of welcome, and spent like there was no tomorrow.

The telephone rang rather insistently, much to Veronica's annoyance, as she was saying farewell to Naseem. 'Please answer that infernal phone, Cindy. There are times in this life when one could see the bloody thing far enough, but it is an essential part of life and business, I know' she said with a shrug.

'Veronica, I think that you had better come to the phone,' Cindy said, rather shaken looking.

'Can't you handle it? I am trying to thank Naseem for the wonderful luncheon,' came the reply and she continued walking him to the door.

'No, I think you will want to answer this call yourself.'

'Really, Cindy!' Veronica said in exasperation. 'Surely you can perform a simple task without having to insist that ...' She stopped in mid-sentence as she turned and saw the expression on Cindy's face. 'What is it Cindy? What on earth is wrong?' Her heart sank

Brainse Bhaile Thormod
Ballyfermot Library
Tel. 6269324/5

to the soles of her feet as apprehension gripped its icy fingers tightly round the knot that was forming in her tummy.

'Please come to the phone, dear,' replied Cindy in a soft voice.

Gingerly, Veronica picked up the receiver. 'Hello,' she said in whisper. 'Yes, this is she.' A few moments later, she replaced the instrument. Ashen, she turned, her eyes glazed. She opened her mouth to say something and then fainted. Cindy stood rooted to the spot as her friend collapsed in a heap at her feet.

'What on earth has happened, Cindy?' Naseem asked as she rushed to Veronica's aid.

'Phillip has been in an accident. I don't know what happened. I only know that he is in hospital in Dundee. The hospital found Veronica's phone number amongst his effects. That is all I know – I don't even know how serious it is. Oh Naseem … we simply must do something!'

'How long does it take to drive to Dundee?'

'I am not even too sure exactly where Dundee is. I know it is in Scotland somewhere,' Cindy blurted, her eyes filling with tears.

'Dundee is on the east coast of Scotland. Don't worry – I'll arrange transport.' He produced a mobile phone from his jacket, dialling as he spoke. A few moments later he rang off after giving instructions delivered in rapidly spoken Arabic and gave Cindy a comforting smile. 'Everything is in hand. The doctor is on his way to attend to Veronica and Ahmid is making the necessary travel arrangements as we speak. Now, be a dear and put the kettle on. I am sure that the first thing Veronica shall require when she comes round is a cup of tea.' He flashed a dazzling white smile and said: 'you know the English – the first step in solving a crisis is the obligatory cup of tea!'

Cindy did as she was bade, pale and quite dazed, obviously very upset. Suddenly she turned to Naseem, as if struck by some profound thought. 'I think that Veronica would prefer a cup of coffee rather than tea. Do you think that that will be alright?'

'I'm sure it will be just perfect,' he replied in a soft sympathetic tone. The shop door opened and the local doctor entered. A quick whiff of smelling salts, and the unconscious Veronica coughed and spluttered as she returned to reality.

Forty minutes later, Veronica found herself in a helicopter on her way north to Dundee. Naseem had had the helicopter at Leeds airport, where he had intended to fly down to London to board his private jet to fly home the following day. Phillip's accident had changed all that, and now he thanked Allah that the machine had been so nearby when most needed.

'I don't know how to thank you,' Veronica began. 'I just do not know wha ...'

Naseem raised his hand, stopping her in mid-sentence. 'There is nothing to thank me for, my dear, I am only too pleased to be of service. Phillip is my friend too, and I would move heaven and earth to be with him at a time like this. I know this is all too easy to say, but please try and not worry too much, Veronica. Phillip is strong, and I am sure receiving the very best medical attention. Allah will look after him, I am sure.' He smiled and gave her hand a reassuring squeeze.

'Thanks. I hope you are right.' She forced a little smile. 'In fact, I know that you are. Oh no!' she said in anguish 'I forgot to ask Cindy to notify Phillip's parents of the accident.'

'All taken care of. I telephoned myself, and they should arrive in Dundee about an hour or so after us,' Naseem replied and Veronica's expression relaxed, showing her relief.

Twenty minutes later the helicopter touched down in the grounds of Ninewells hospital in the city of Dundee. A few words from the right people, and the rules were relaxed for the Sultan of Qazan's personal flight to land in the hospital grounds. Safety of his royal personage and courtesy was the criteria of the day, the trustees of Ninewells having been advised by the Foreign Office to extend full cooperation to his Highness. Naseem knew only too well that the large pool of oil that lay under the sand of his country commanded political respect far outweighing its importance. He silently praised Allah for His blessings.

Chapter Eleven

The next forty-eight hours were fraught with anxiety. Phillip had slipped on a rock on the final day of filming, and fractured his skull. He had to have major surgery to relieve a build-up of pressure on the brain caused by internal haemorrhaging. The operation had gone well, but there remained a danger that the bleeding could recur due to the severity of the damage to his cranium sustained in the fall. Mr Fraser, the neurosurgeon who had performed the surgery, informed them that until Phillip regained consciousness, he could not rule out the possibility of brain damage. The thought of such a catastrophe befalling her beloved Phillip was almost more than Veronica could bear.

Naseem had been a tower of strength during this period, keeping everyone's spirits up when they were at their lowest ebb. Phillip's parents had arrived shortly after she and Naseem. They were naturally extremely worried about their son, and Veronica knew that they were more than slightly perplexed as to what she was doing there, and exactly what relationship she had with Phillip, but too polite to say so. She felt slightly awkward in their company – after all, she would have found it nigh near impossible to explain their platonic relationship to them, and make it sound plausible as to what she was actually doing at his bedside. How on earth could she tell them that she was in love with him, but that as far as she was aware, the feeling was one sided?

Cindy had arrived in Dundee the day after Veronica, having arranged with her dad to tend the shop. He had agreed at once, which Veronica thought was extremely admirable. He was, when all was said and done, one of the most successful businessmen in

Australia, and it really was quite magnificent of him to make such a magnanimous gesture. Cindy merely said that she would never have spoken to him again if he had refused. After all, he did enjoy the privilege of being her parent. And helping out when needed came with the territory. But she did concede that he wasn't a bad old soul, really, but threatened Veronica within an inch of her life if she ever told him that she had said so.

The days dragged by, one into another, or so it seemed to Veronica. Phillip still showed no signs of regaining consciousness, and everyone was becoming more worried, with the exception of the medical staff, who patiently explained that different people take different time periods to regain consciousness – trying their very best to reassure everyone.

Naseem and Phillip's father spoke several times, considering whether to have Phillip transferred to a clinic in Switzerland, but to his credit, the Swiss consultant assured them that Phillip was receiving the very best medical care available in Ninewells. Communication had been by way of satellite TV link, but second thoughts led them to decide on a face-to-face meeting. They both flew to Switzerland to reassure themselves that Herr Hiller fully understood Phillip's situation. They returned to Dundee having agreed that he would be flown to Geneva if he did not show signs of full normality when consciousness did return.

The days dragged past with no change in his condition. Worry was etched deeply into each and every face. Anxiety was now slowly yielding to a feeling of depression, and an odd moment found each suffering from mild panic attacks. Even Cindy was becoming more silent as time relentlessly marched on its interminable way, dreadfully unforgiving to those who waited, and worried, and prayed.

Veronica sat at Phillip's bedside during the long nights, stroking his face and talking to him, pouring out her heart for him, wondering at times if he heard her voice or was even aware of her presence. The doctors had said that the sound of a familiar voice could sometimes trigger a response in the patient, and she was only too glad to try. The thought that he might actually be able to hear what she was saying to him would make her self-conscious, and she would temper her conversation to current events and how the shop was doing. Then she would forget herself and proclaim her love once more. It was almost too much to bear at times, and she would retreat to the corridor and silently weep.

On the third night, she was keeping her vigil, talking of her love, and fantasising what their children would turn out like. Would they he tall, or would they only be average height? She then stated emphatically that they would be tall, with their father's blond hair – she simply would not settle for anything less! Suddenly, she became self-conscious that she was being watched, and turned her head quickly. To her great embarrassment, Mrs Marden was standing at her side. She blushed to her roots, like a schoolgirl caught smoking behind the bike shed.

'I knew it – I just knew it. You two are having a secret romance! You are obviously very much in love, my dear.' His mother smiled sweetly as she spoke, and then she gave Veronica a loving hug and a kiss on her cheek.

'I … I don't really know what to say,' she stammered. 'I must admit that I do love your son, but I am rather afraid that it is one sided and … and well, I would not want you to jump to the wrong conclusion. Phillip really is a very good friend, and on his part, I am no more. I am very embarrassed. I never meant for anyone to overhear.

Please promise that you won't tell him what I have been saying to him when he recovers?' she pleaded, her eyes filling involuntarily.

'Oh, my dear Veronica, please forgive me. I never intended to cause you hurt. I am a very silly woman – I did not mean to spy. But when I heard you pour your love for my son from the depth of your heart, I simply could not interrupt you. I know that it was extremely rude of me to eavesdrop, and I cannot apologise enough. Phillip is my son, and it would be untrue of me to say that I did not take a certain delight to witness your love for him. A mother worries about a son's welfare, and the women in his life. I must confess that I was delighted to learn that you two loved each other. At least that was my assumption, but it would seem that I did indeed jump to the wrong conclusion and I can only say more fool Phillip! You are a charming person, loving and caring, and I cannot imagine for a moment why he has not swept you in his arms before some other man does.' Her face was flushed after her long heartfelt speech, and she was feeling more than a little guilty for her conduct. She knew that it was unforgivable, and goodness only knew what her husband would say if he ever learned of her misdeed.

Veronica studied Mrs Marden's face for a second, not quite knowing what to say, then suddenly she put her arms around her neck and whispered that there was nothing to forgive. 'I do love Phillip,' she said, 'but I decided a long time ago that his friendship would have to suffice. I never meant to spill my feeling for him quite so audibly, so I have only myself to blame. I would die if I thought for one moment that he could actually hear what I have been saying to him the past few nights. You don't think that is possible, do you?'

'I honestly do not know, my dear, but I fervently hope that he has heard, and understood every utterance. Perhaps it is just what he needs to goad him into action.'

She smiled a broad smile, put her arm around Veronica, and suggested that they go for a much-needed and well-deserved cup of tea.

Over the next few days, Veronica and Mrs Marden became firm friends, bonded by their mutual love for Phillip. Naseem had to return to his country for a period of two days, the burdens of State being too great to ignore. He had a very heavy heart when he left, promising to return as soon as possible, if not before, he had added.

Special permission was granted him by the Foreign Office and Ministry of Defence for his private Lear jet to land at RAF Leuchars, the nearest runway long enough to accommodate the aircraft's take-off requirement.

Phillip had shown no improvement during this period and the only ones not showing signs of extreme anxiety were the medical staff. The doctors did their best to reassure one and all, with great patience and courtesy, that a coma was very unpredictable, and that the patient could recover consciousness when least expected, and to never to lose hope.

On the fifth night, Veronica was keeping her vigil at her beloved's bedside, where she was joined by Ann Marden. After a while, his mother had insisted on a first-name basis, which Veronica was grateful for. Ann had brought a welcome cup of coffee for them, and they sipped it, chatting quietly about Naseem and the influence he had to be granted permission to land his plane at an RAF base.

'What time is it?'

'Just gone half past two,' Veronica replied, glancing at her watch. And then the penny dropped. 'Phillip!' she gasped. Ann dropped her cup, spilling coffee over the bedcover.'Where am I?' he asked in a slightly husky voice.

'You are in hospital,' they answered in unison, and then both the women started to laugh, tears of joy streaming down their faces.

'How long have I been here?'

'Five days. Five very long days,' his mother replied.

Veronica pressed the buzzer to summon the staff as Ann spoke, and a young intern appeared as if by magic. He spoke quietly to Phillip, examining him all the while.

'Welcome back to the world – you have been a very lucky man. Everything seems to be in working order. I want you to have a rest now, so don't keep him awake too long please, ladies.' He smiled, and added that he would look in again in a short while.

Phillip slept the rest of the night, but both Veronica and his mother stayed with him, ever anxious that he might relapse back into the coma. They had, of course, informed everyone that he had regained consciousness, but on the doctor's insistence, no one else was allowed in to see him until he had slept properly.

Early next morning, all anxiety dissolved when Phillip wakened and declared that he was famished, and asked when breakfast was served in this establishment, winking and smiling all the while at Veronica.

Everyone duly arrived at his bedside, crying, laughing and celebrating Phillip's recovery. Naseem arrived later that morning, and rushed to see Phillip for himself. The TV crew did an impromptu interview at the bedside, and incorporated the segment into the programme they were filming when the accident happened. 'No point wasting a great human interest story when it presents itself on a plate,' the director observed, just as the consultant dropped by to check on his patient. To say he hit the roof would be putting it rather mildly, and the TV cameras and sound equipment were sent from the room forthwith in no small hurry.

Everyone stayed on another day, and then Veronica and Cindy decided that they had better return to the shop. After all, poor Tom had gallantly remained holding the fort, for no personal financial gain whatsoever, and Veronica especially did not want to feel that she was playing on his good nature.

She would forever he in his debt for what he had so selflessly done; and Naseem immediately offered the services of his helicopter to facilitate their speedy return home.

It was with a heavy heart that Veronica prepared to leave, and with a mix of despondency and utter relief at his recovery that she bade Phillip farewell. He thanked her kindly for coming to see him, (rather formally, she thought) and then said that he would pop in to visit as soon as he got some spare time, and then shook her hand. It was with an extremely sad heart indeed that she boarded the helicopter, trying not to show her disappointment and hurt to the others as they waved goodbye. Ann kissed her on the cheek, and promised to make a point of dropping in to see her the journey back down south. She clasped Veronica tightly, and slipped a gold St Christopher into her hand, whispering that it was to ensure a safe journey, and a small thank you for all she had done for her son. Veronica was almost overcome with emotion, but bravely fought back her tears, and stepped quickly into the aircraft.

Soft warm raindrops caressed Veronica's face as she made her way to open the shop some two weeks later. Phillip had phoned her to thank her once again for her care, and explained that he was going to Canada for a short break with Naseem to recuperate, and that he would be in to visit when he returned. She was glad that his recovery was complete, and that he had not suffered any setbacks, but she did so yearn to see him once more.

She sighed a big sigh as she turned the key in the lock, and opened the door to begin yet another day's trading. Cindy was taking the day off to go with Greg to see a bungalow that they had seen advertised in the *Yorkshire Post* the previous evening. The thought that they might soon he leaving saddened Veronica, but it was an inevitable fact that she would have to face sooner or later.

She had grown accustomed to their company, and she just knew that she would especially miss Cindy – she was such good fun to have around. One simply never knew from one day to the next just what she would do or say. She was simply unpredictable, her sense of humour being truly legendary.

A hot cup of coffee started the day as normal, once the till was set up and the float counted and deposited in the drawer. The postman came at his usual time, and Veronica was rather delighted to receive a letter from her supplier informing her that her order for the pewter tankards was well in hand, and would be delivered on time as promised.

This piece of news brightened her mood no end, and she hummed softly to herself as she made another coffee. Her thoughts drifted inevitably to Phillip, and she wondered for the umpteenth time what he was doing, and how he was feeling. She knew that his experience must have had a lasting effect on him, no matter what he said. No one could go through that without it telling on them and she worried that he was taking care, and resting as he was instructed to do. But knowing him, she figured that he was probably doing the opposite.

The morning went slowly, with only a few brave souls daring to venture out into the rain. Around eleven, a coach pulled in to the parking lot and some intrepid tourists braved the elements and made their way to the shop. They were mainly elderly Americans, doing the Grand Tour (Britain and Europe) and they spent quite freely. This was the end of their trip, and they seemed all too anxious to be rid of the Sterling in their pockets. Veronica was quite amazed to discover that it was well after twelve o'clock when the last couple exited the shop.

The kettle was put to boil, and she prepared herself a sandwich. She had brought some cold chicken-breast slices with her in the morning, knowing that she would not have the opportunity to leave the shop in order to purchase something for lunch. She was quite peckish by then, and the chicken tasted rather delicious, so much so that she decided to be a glutton and have another one.

Ann Marden had not visited her as yet, and Veronica wondered if all was well with her and her husband. She liked Ann a lot, and they had become firm friends in the short time they had been at the hospital, and it really puzzled her as to why she had not heard from her. She did hope that they were not suffering any ill effects from the strain of Phillip's accident. The pressure must have been unbearable on them, and she knew that stress could have disastrous consequences at times. She scolded herself severely for being such a pessimist and gave herself a good talking to on the subject of positive thinking.

'Of course everything is fine with Ann and her husband!' she said aloud to her reflection in the front shop window. Two bicycles drew up in front of the shop, the riders wearing rainproof capes around their shoulders and helmets coloured vivid red to match the capes were securely fastened with Lycra straps clipped under their chins. Veronica found the sight comical yet sad at the same time. They did look so funny in the bright clothing and yet had all the appearance of feeling utterly miserable too. Rainwater was dripping down their bare legs, onto the seemingly compulsory vivid red cycling shoes. Their legs were mud streaked, and sweat poured freely down their faces. They really did look the picture of abject misery!

When they entered the shop, Veronica sympathised about what a terrible day it was for cycling, only to be told it was all part and parcel of the joys of cycling, and the English weather was what made the holiday so interesting. They were having a great time, thank you very much, and did not need some yokel's sympathy. And with that tirade, they stormed out. Veronica was absolutely stunned, and left wondering what she had said to annoy them so. She shrugged, and put it down to the weather.

About twenty minutes later, the sound of a helicopter shattered the tranquillity of the village, as its rotors fought valiantly against the heavy moisture-laden air in an effort to secure a safe and gentle landing. She rushed to the window. Yes – it was Naseem's helicopter. The door of the aircraft opened, and Phillip jumped jauntily down to the ground. Her heart leapt for joy.

He came up the street at a jog, blond hair blowing in the breeze. Veronica's eyes never left him for a moment. She had missed him so! As he approached the shop, he suddenly, and quite inexplicably, veered across the street, and went directly into the hotel. Veronica was astounded, puzzled, and shattered by his action. She had naturally assumed that he had come to visit her. She suddenly felt foolish. Phillip had obviously business to conduct in the hotel, and it had been extremely presumptuous of her to take it for granted he had come specially to see her. Nevertheless, a tiny tear managed to trickle from the comer of her eye and she had to admit that she was more than a little hurt.

A few minutes later, the situation became even more puzzling when Phillip came from the hotel accompanied by the manager, and they came at a run to the shop.

'Hi Veronica – don't have time to explain, but Jim has kindly agreed to look after the shop for a while. Now be a good girl, and put on your coat and come with me,' he said, or rather, commanded.

'What? You expect me to up and leave everything at the drop of a hat, just like that, Phillip Marden, without as much as an explanation? You know that I cannot simply walk out of the shop whenever it takes my fancy – I have a business to run. What on earth is wrong? Are your parents alright? Nothing has happened to them, I hope.'

'No. Nothing has happened to my parents, or anyone else for that matter, Veronica, I promise you. It is just that I need you to come with me. Now, you will have to trust me – time is of the essence. Please don't let us argue, just put on a coat and come.' He took her hands in his and squeezed them gently. 'If the weather worsens the chopper will be grounded, so be a dear and please hurry.'

Mesmerised, Veronica did as he asked, and donned her coat. Before she realised what was happening, she was on board the helicopter and leaving terra firma behind, in a great whirl of rain and mud. 'Where are we going?' And why on earth do you need my presence so much? I just don't understand, Phillip. Please explain.'

'All in good time, Veronica. Let's take time to catch our breaths. We are very lucky, you know. The pilot told me if we had been much longer, we would indeed have been grounded. Naseem sends his regards, and his apologies that he could not come with me. Pressures of State and all that, you know,' he replied, smiling warmly.

Veronica's brain was racing. Why was Phillip being so secretive, evasive, and indeed infuriating? She glanced out the window, trying to gather her thoughts. All she could see was grey mist. Suddenly, they broke through the cloud, and the azure of the sky and brightness of the sun was almost blinding. Looking down, the cloud reminded her of cotton wool though even more pristine white, she reflected. Abruptly, her thoughts returned to why she was up in the sky in the first place, and she turned her attention back to the cause of her being there.

'I really would appreciate some straight answers, Phillip. Why have you dragged me from my business and whisked me off in a helicopter to who knows where? You surely must realise that the situation is quite ludicrous, if not exasperating.'

'I know. This is a situation that you must take on trust, Veronica. All I can say is that I promise that nothing is amiss. You have my word on that. Please trust me.' Once more his amazing blue eyes burned into her, and she simply melted. She had no defence against them – how utterly infuriating!

A few breaks began to appear in the cloud, and she could see green fields below. The hills had disappeared, and the ground seemed to be flatter. She had no idea where they were, and Phillip simply evaded the question with the skill of a polished politician. She decided is give up and play along with him. Stupid men's games he, Tim, and undoubtedly Greg played all the time, and everyone else had to join in at their behest. 'Men!' she mumbled to herself.

'What was that? I didn't catch you with the noise of the engine.'

'Nothing!' she said. 'I was just talking in myself, trying to figure out in which direction we are flying.' She blushed with shame as she lied.

'Aha – we are here,' Phillip announced, smiling widely.

Veronica looked out, and saw a village rapidly coming into view as they descended. There was something familiar about it but she just could not put a name to it. But she knew she had seen it before, either in person or in a photograph. Places looked somewhat different from the air.

The helicoper touched down without so much as a bump, and Phillip jumped nimbly and raised his arms to help Veronica.

'Where are we?' she asked as her feet touched terra firma once more. And then she saw, to her astonishment, Elizabeth and Tim, Cindy and Greg, Tom, Naseem and Phillip's parents, and to her complete amazement, her mother, stepfather and her sister.

'Gretna Green,' Phillip replied.

'What? I … I'm sorry. Phillip. What did you say?' she stammered.

'I said, we are in Gretna Green.'

'Gretna Green! What on earth are we doing in Gretna Green? And why is everyone here?' She looked very puzzled.

'How very remiss of me. I am sorry. Didn't I tell you? We are going to a wedding!' he replied, smiling.

'You know very well that you didn't tell me, Phillip Marden,' she retorted, feeling quite miffed.

'How do you expect me to attend a wedding? I am not dressed for a wedding!' she fumed.

'Don't worry your pretty little head about that – it has all been all taken care of.' He was still grinning much to the now raging Veronica's annoyance.

'Oh, it is, is it? And by the way. I forgot to ask, just whose wedding is it anyway?' she snapped, her eyes blazing daggers.

'Didn't I say? Why … ours, of course!' Before she could say anything, she was in his arms and lost in the warmth of his kiss, the cheers of family and friends ringing in her ears.

THE END

You may also enjoy...

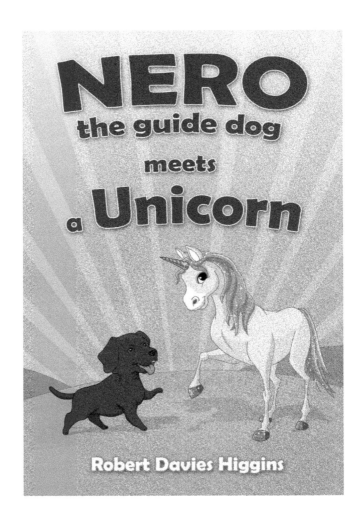

Lightning Source UK Ltd.
Milton Keynes UK
UKHW03f0701150418
321065UK00001B/18/P

9 781785 386084